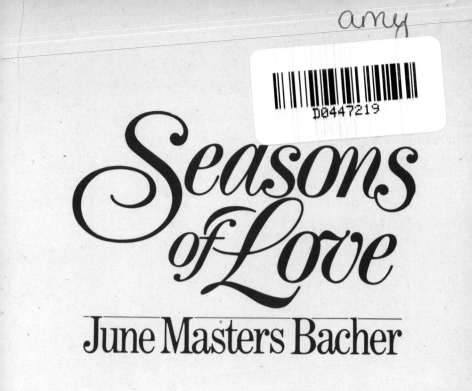

amy

Seasons of Love

June Masters Bacher

HARVEST HOUSE PUBLISHERS
Eugene, Oregon 97402

Other Books by June Masters Bacher:

Dreams Beyond Tomorrow
Love Is a Gentle Stranger
Love's Silent Song
Diary of a Loving Heart
Love Leads Home
Journey To Love
Echoes From the Past
The Heart That Lingers
Until There Was You
When Love Shines Through
With All My Heart
A Mother's Joy
Kitchen Delights
Quiet Moments for Women

Scripture quotations are from the King James Version of the Bible.

SEASONS OF LOVE

Copyright © 1986 by Harvest House Publishers
Eugene, Oregon 97402

ISBN 0-89081-504-6

Printed in the United States of America.

To:
Carol & Wayne Campbell
Lou & Jiggs Falls
Anne & David Hein
Lucke & Bob Miller
Lee & Bill Turner

For the SEASONS OF LOVE we have shared!

—June & George Bacher

Dear, Amy
I hope you enjoy
this book. I hope you
make as many good
friends as you are to
me! I Love You alot
write me alot of
letters

Love
Ya
Loanna

PREFACE

Nature has carefully arranged—as if by Divine Hand—that Oregon should be the last region on the continent for the white man to enter. Mountains stand guard to the south and east and north. On the west is a rugged coast.

Because of its blend of sunshine and showers, Oregon is the land of rainbows. And chasing rainbows brought adventurous, gold-seeking Spaniards close to the Oregon shores. But the mountains turned them back. There was a shrug of their shoulders and a decision that there probably was no gold in the New World after all . . .

Frontier life was hard, but dream-filled, for the early settlers who brought the first wagon trains over the mountains. And the Almighty would understand if they occasionally gave in to whispers of "Gold!"

SEASONS OF LOVE (primarily fiction) will touch a few home bases of reality geographically and historically. And, yes, for you more adventuresome travelers, there *is* a "Blue Bucket Mine" . . . and it remains lost to this day.

A sequel to JOURNEY TO LOVE and DREAMS BEYOND TOMORROW, SEASONS OF LOVE will take Rachel, Cole, and all the other characters you came to know in the previous books to the mine and its mysteries. Join them in their quest, their love, and their faith—the greatest treasure of all!

—June Masters Bacher

CONTENTS

To every thing there is a season, and
a time to every purpose under the heaven:
A time to be born, and a time to die;
a time to plant, and a time to pluck. . .
A time to weep, and a time to laugh;
a time to mourn, and a time to dance. . .
A time to embrace, and a time to refrain from
embracing. . .
A time to keep silence, and a time to speak;
A time to love, and a time to hate;
a time of war, and a time of peace. . .
He hath made every thing beautiful in his time:
also he hath set the world in their heart, so that
no man can find out the work that God maketh from
the beginning to the end.

—Ecclesiastes 3:1-11

1

A Time To Mourn

The snow flurries twirled into the valley unexpectedly—early in the season, like everything else that was happening in her life. November should instead be warm with color.

Rachel pushed back the yellow-checked curtains for a better view from the kitchen window. It was only a few paces from the cabin to the Meeting House which served temporarily as a school. The fiercely-independent Star looked after herself well. But from force of habit Rachel watched. Maybe it was the ghost of the other child—the one she had never known—that caused her to be so over-protective of this six-year-old who had come to her as mysteriously from the Unknown as her own infant daughter had been sucked into it. Hers and Cole's. Their lasting link . . .

Would things have been different if the baby had lived? Rachel sighed heavily, letting the curtains slip through her numb fingers. Automatically, she left the window to lay another log on the fire. But her mind was on the ever-widening chasm between herself and her husband. When had the first warning crack appeared? And how had she failed to notice? Once he was gentle, sweet, and understanding. While now . . .

To get away from the "now" of things, Rachel thought back to the early days of their two-year marriage. Not arranged in heaven, she remembered, but as their love grew, the shadow of how the marriage came to be slunk away. And they were in love the way Rachel had thought happened only in a dream or a Bronte novel.

Loving Cole as she did, Rachel had never doubted that he could build this square of Oregon wilderness into the city as he dreamed. In her eyes, he simply plucked a handful of stars from the sky and shaped them to fit God's plan. His dream became hers. Every common pebble encased a possible lump of pure gold.

Togetherness. That is what they had then—even when they were apart. And now they were miles apart even when they were together. Did Cole miss the excitement, the challenge, the *love*? He never talked about it.

Sighing again, Rachel took a loaf of graham bread from the cupboard, sliced a piece, and buttered it. It was past supper time and Star must be hungry. Besides, life had to go on. Even when the stars she and Cole once gathered so easily now streaked across the heavens, leaving her spirits as dark as the vacant place created by their fall.

Rachel checked the window again, a little uneasily. The low-hanging clouds, an ominous gray, spat out little, scattered flakes sullenly.

Aunt Em, who had proven to be more mother than friend along the Applegate Trail and here in the settlement, would have blamed Rachel's depression—like her own neuralgia—on the weather.

Both of them knew better. Things were not right between her and Cole. How, she wondered now, could a husband who loved his wife insist on a return to something he called "normal" after her loss? Couldn't he see her as she was—a broken shell from whom life had stolen the pearl? He did not understand—or even try to—how empty she felt, how hollowed out inside. Just as he was unable to understand that she could not risk another hurt so soon.

"It's *not* soon, Rachel," Cole had said last night. His tone was reasonable. His words were not. "Three months is not too soon—"

"One does not measure grief in terms of time." Rachel's voice was flat and lifeless, like her body.

"But, my darling, Star has needs. *I* have needs. There will be other children." When Cole reached out to her, Rachel turned away from the inviting circle of his arms.

"No!" The word hung there between them. More than a refusal, it was a denial of his needs. Of his love. Of life itself.

Rachel had crawled into bed rigid with a nameless anger. What was it Paul told the Ephesians? "Let not the sun go down on your wrath." But an apology was no good without repentance and a change.

Oh, Lord, her heart cried out in the darkness, *I am not ready yet!* And so she had lain motionless beside Cole—so stiff and unrelenting that her bones ached with fatigue. She had not slept. But she feigned slumber when she heard him get up and fumble for his clothes in the predawn darkness, careful not to awaken her. He would be away all day, he had said last night—something to do with another land grant.

There was a moment when he leaned over her. Maybe if he kissed her . . . but he did not. Instead, he tiptoed out, closing the door quietly and latching it behind him.

Rachel had lain there remembering with an awful ache the baby she, Cole, and Star had wanted so much . . . counting the months, then the days as the horseshoe of buildings, a town in its infancy, was repaired after the Indian raid and a heavier stockade erected around it. As the buildings took shape, the miracle of life took shape beneath her heart. And time marched on. The river thawed. The lilacs bloomed. And the early peaches blushed beneath the ripening June sun.

"It's almost time," Cole said over and over, holding Rachel tenderly, kissing her hair, and teasing her about a name for their new baby.

Those had been happy days. "Why, Colby, of course. Colby Lord, Jr." Rachel had said, so certain was she that the child she carried would be a son.

Star was unconvinced. "We will have a girl-child," she insisted in the way Rachel and Cole had come to expect. It was as if this child of theirs occasionally reentered the world from which she had emerged. A world neither of her adopted parents understood. "Lorraine, please. The name stands for the cross of Jesus."

But little Lorraine was now "Angel Baby" to Estrellita, their Star. The beautiful infant took one breath and then she was gone. Her departure left Cole and Star saddened but wanting to comfort Rachel, who refused to be consoled. She wanted to escape as her baby had escaped, to stop living . . .

The front door slammed. Rachel turned quickly to greet Star. "You're half-frozen, darling—"

But Star's face was aglow with a strange light. "God made a snowflake blanket for Angel Baby," she whispered.

Rachel was too overcome to reply. She simply

reached out her arms to Star and drew the child's wispy sweetness to her heart. Tears, her first, flowed freely.

What was it Aunt Em had said? "Even marriage has its seasons, dearie. Sunshine 'n rain cause life's rainbows." Occasional storms following one-time warmth did not mean the end of love then? Maybe there was a purpose for the cycle of the seasons. Yes, there must be. God arranged it. So He understood her need of a time to mourn.

2

A Time To Keep Silent

Supper over, Star and Moreover, the monstrous, blue-gray Irish wolfhound who was her shadow, stretched out in front of the open fireplace. Star's little brown fingers squeezed a piece of charcoal.

Pushing the cloud of black hair from her pixie face, the child looked up at Rachel. "I am drawing the snow, Mother Mine," she said. "But it keeps melting away." Paper poised in midair, "Are there winters in heaven, I wonder?" Star asked without a change in expression.

Rachel felt bewilderment etch her face. How did one deal with this Miracle Child? "Maybe it's always spring."

"No snow? No rain? Then there would be no rainbows. We should not like that. No?"

Star seemed to be addressing the dog, but her words lingered with Rachel. Maybe in expecting all sunshine, one missed the glow of Star and Aunt Em's rainbows. But Rachel could do with fewer storms.

Uneasily, she peered out the window again. Had Cole said when to expect him home?

Admittedly, she was a poor listener of late, locked as she was into her private world of grief.

The world outside the window was dark. She could see only patches of white in the path of the lamplight and her own reflection in the glass. Instinctively, while trying to ignore a persistent spark of worry, Rachel touched her hair—tucking a stray curl here and there beneath the wheat-gold of the braid encircling her head. Her hair and the little sift of freckles across her nose remained as they had been when she first met Cole. But the rest of her had changed. The rounded innocence of girl-hood, the bright-eyed expectancy, the impulsive but appealingly helpless gestures were gone. They were replaced by a tightly wound look. And in her hazel eyes there was an expression of waiting.

Waiting. That had been the story of her marriage. Waiting to reach the end of the trail. Waiting for Cole to come home from his endless string of business trips . . . to resume the honeymoon which they never finished . . . to resume their life. Waiting for the baby. Waiting, *waiting* . . .

Buck ("Buckeye" Jones, the Wagon Master on the trail—now Mr. Jones, Financial Manager of Cole's growing town) had noticed the change. Ever the faithful friend, "I'm worried about you and Cole," he had said, the concern in his voice reflecting in the earth-toned eyes. "It's a tremendous task Cole has undertaken."

"*Too* tremendous?" Buck, her human wailing wall and "uncle" (almost father) to Star during Cole's absences, was always open to her questions and honest in his answers.

"No," Buck had answered. Cole could handle a crisis. "Comes from his great faith, the combination of a cool head, yet so caring. He'll handle things unless—"

When he hesitated, Rachel felt he wanted to say more. Not knowing how to ask, she kept silent. When at length he spoke, the words were more personal.

"His qualifications are the best. Like his stallion, he can take all the hills. It's something more—something I can't put a finger on. He's too sharply honed, almost waiting for the close shave he knows will come. While you, Rachel—"

"Yes, Buck? What am I like?"

Buck sucked in his breath, reached for one of her hands and stroked it absently, then laid it back in her lap. "You're overtired, Rachel." He paused and attempted to smile. "Let's say you're like a wick that's trimmed too closely—getting dangerously near the oil—ready to explode."

The word surprised her. "With *you*?"

This time Buck's smile was more successful. "Not with me—more with Cole. The two I love the most. There! I've said too much."

No, not too much. This gentle friend had said no more than she herself knew. There had been too many crises. Too many postponements. Too many disappointments. These, not the hard work, accounted for the smile on Rachel's lips which never quite reached her eyes, the attempted laugh which came out hollow and forced. It had never occurred to her that these might be signs of disaster. If she snapped, Cole snapped. *That* would be disaster.

Disaster meant losing Cole. *Oh, dear God, no!* Rachel's heart cried out at the thought. That tiny spark within her was now a blazing fire. If the snow kept up, the roads would be a graveyard of white. Cole might be lost somewhere in need of help. Trembling with tension and cold, Rachel reached for Cole's heavy wool coat that hung on a peg by the door and was about to slip her arms into it when she stopped. The idea of getting Buck and searching for her husband was foolish when she had no idea where he was supposed to be.

As she hung the coat back in its familiar place, another thought—so foreign to Rachel that at first she refused to acknowledge it—clawed at her heart.

Was Cole angry with her about last night? Had she perhaps taken one step too far? It was possible for a woman to lose the man she loved in ways other than snowstorms. She remembered accounts her mother had given long ago about seafaring men like her father who left their homes in the morning and never returned. And by the way Mother told the stories Rachel had known the men were not lost at sea. . . .

Now, suddenly, Rachel found herself jerking the coat down again and thrusting her arms inside, driven by a force she did not understand.

"I'm going to look for Daddy, Star," Rachel began. But she was never able to finish outlining her plan of searching alone.

"Then you will need a hunting dog. Come, *Perro*, let us seek my father." Star was shrugging into a jacket.

And suddenly the three of them were pushing through the night, concentrating on avoiding the deeper spots of snow. Where would they look for Cole? None of them knew. Consequently, there was no conversation. But sometimes, as Aunt Em put it, there can be "talk without words." So, in wordless communication, they knew they would be guided to find the man they loved.

They moved silently through the shadows and made the turn toward the Meeting House as if by mutual agreement. The dog nosed ahead. Rachel clung hard to Star's cold, little fingers. And somehow through it all, Rachel was conscious that the snow had stopped. The moon, slipping from behind dark clouds, smiled brightly in the brilliant caldron of stars. "Is it not beautiful, Mother Mine?" Little Star whispered. Rachel nodded, clutching the small hand tighter, unable to speak.

And then ahead, illuminated by the glow of the gold-rimmed moon, three figures loomed into view. One of them—*Oh, praise the Lord!*—was Cole. Moreover barked and ran ahead. Star broke away, her small feet hastily high-jumping the slippery mounds.

"Dad-*dee, Dad-dee!*" The silver-bell sweetness of the child's voice tinkled across the crisp night air.

Relief swept over Rachel with such force that her legs felt weak beneath her. And yet the heart inside her had never felt so strong. What did it matter who the other men were or what the nature of their business might be? The terrible nightmare was over. She was Colby Lord's wife and the love she felt for him had been too long denied. Cole was home. Cole was safe. Cole was *hers!*

So thinking, Rachel, too, was running. She reached Cole's side, too breathless to speak. It was enough for now just to be consumed with happiness, the kind that made winter, with all its attempted foreverness, unable to chill the springtime in her heart.

I was worried. . .I was afraid you would not come back to me. . .I thought. . .Oh, Cole, I love you. . .

These words her heart cried out inside, even as she shook hands with the two men whose names she failed to catch when Cole introduced them. Cole had taken hold of her arm. She thrilled like a schoolgirl at its warm possessiveness.

"The hotel is not ready for occupancy yet," Cole

explained. "But do you think it could accommodate our guests—"

"Oh, yes!" Her enthusiasm must have surprised Cole for she felt a quick jerk of his head. A little embarrassed, Rachel went on, "There are bunks and Aunt Em is prepared to serve breakfast."

Even as she murmured the proper words of welcome, Rachel was keenly aware of Cole's eyes on her there in the silvery light of the November moon. Not only did she feel his gray-green eyes, she knew the message spelled out in their deep translucency. It said that Cole had seen the change. That he knew what was in her heart. And that Cole, being Cole, would never make her say the words.

"I will bring blankets," Rachel said, not wishing to sound rude but wishing with all her heart that these men would turn toward the largest of the buildings on the half-circle bend of the growing city. Once the guests were quartered, she and Cole could be together.

But the men seemed to be in no hurry. "I understand your new house is underway—a much larger one?"

Yes, Rachel said. And, yes, it would be nice—nice, too, to vacate the close quarters the settlers had occupied, each building a cabin and proving up on a claim, in order for places of business to open in the vacated space.

"We will need those businesses—likely to flourish, eh, Cole?" the other man said. And before her husband could answer, the man burst out with his news. "You see, Mrs. Lord, we suspect there's gold in the old quarry."

Gold at Superstition Mountain. Incredible! But Rachel's heart was praising God for restored oneness with Cole. So she was silent.

3

A Time To Embrace

To the west the paling moon retired discreetly behind the towering firs. To the east, the first exploratory fingers of a pink dawn caressed the mountain peaks. And still they talked. It was, Rachel thought, almost as if she and Cole had just met. As if everything about them, including their love, were new.

In the half-dark she could see the beautiful outline of his face on her pillow—his own as yet left untouched. He held her close, strong fingers stroking the smoothness of her hair, released from its coils to drop to her shoulders the way he liked it best. But she could feel the tension inside him—tension born of excitement. Cole thrived on adventure. Blazing the Oregon Trail. Making preliminary arrangements for the city. And now the search for gold.

"You don't really want me to go through with this, do you, Rachel? Don't you see, darling, what it will mean to the valley in case of a strike?"

Rachel sucked in a silent breath. Even now,

wrapped in the warm security of Cole's arms, she felt a flicker of apprehension. So recently released from the prison of depression, she had wanted to begin anew.

"It's just that I'm selfish, I guess, Cole. I so wanted us to be together and, as you said, to build a family."

Cole's arms tightened around her. "Oh, Rachel, little sweetheart, don't you think I want that, too? What I want for us is a lifetime together. What's a few added trips—"

It was hard to think with his lips brushing hers, blurring out his own words. Even drowning in happiness, Rachel felt herself clutching at his words. "A few added trips," Cole had said. But that meant being torn apart. Only they weren't apart now. They were together, together—*together*. This was a time to embrace, a time to replace foreboding with the jubilation of love.

Secure in that thought, Rachel was asleep almost at once. And the dreams came, the sad memories she had thought erased in the joy of Cole's return. She saw again the loneliness of the Oregon Trail when Cole was too involved to know of Julius Doogan's unwelcome advances...the man's returns, his threats, his taking away little Star. All to retaliate against Cole who had done what he had to do— remove a man who as aide-de-camp was a threat to all. And then in her dream she saw again the crimson clouds above the village the night of the Indian raid, watched Cole's buildings fall to ruin, and heard Agnes Grant's hysterical screams about the "rim of fire that'll destroy us all!" But in the confusing chronology one experiences in a dream, somewhere in those menacing cinders was the baby she had lost...somewhere...somewhere...and there was nobody to share her grief. Cole was gone.

Rachel awoke in a cold sweat. She must have slept

only a few minutes. And Cole had not slept at all. His pillow was still fluffed, his covers neatly turned back. And from somewhere in the close confines of the cabin, she heard the sound of men's subdued voices and the cup-against-saucer clatter that said morning coffee. She could use a cup. But she was bone-weary from lack of sleep and exhausted from the dream. She would stretch...

And then the rapid-fire discussion reached her ears.

"The Oregon folks want to farm, Cole, not cut trees."

"I know." Cole's voice sounded tired. "But, look at it this way, Sam. Wheat's depleting the soil. And now with all the homesteading, the grazing land will be cut up by fences. There'll be friction between cattle and sheep men for control of water holes. We *have* to look to the future."

The man named Sam agreed and then added, "Ponce here can do the surveying. If there's gold, he'll know."

There was a pause in which Rachel supposed Ponce was thinking before he said, "I'll know." The words came without arrogance. Just a simple statement of fact. "But," he cautioned, "it's best at this point that we keep this as quiet as possible, trying to avoid what happened in California—"

The voices dropped low. When they became audible again, it was Cole who spoke. "I feel, however, that we are compelled to warn our neighbors of the 'dummy homesteaders.' They have no intention of making use of the land here, so will be filing on the timber tracts."

"Legal under the law, I'm afraid." Sam's voice.

"*But*," Cole answered quietly, "as soon as they lay hand on the title to the land, they turn it over to the eastern mill owners."

"And that *ain't* legal!" Ponce's voice.

"What we want to avoid is a push to dummy-homestead all the land, because this is home to those of us who have come here to tame a wilderness and hand it down to our children's children as their birthright. And, at all costs, we must try to avoid a gold rush. More coffee?"

Both men said no. "Then join me in prayer," Cole said.

Rachel's heart melted. Cole, wonderful Cole, had reached out and embraced the good of all in his thinking. His tie with the Lord was as elemental as earth and fire.

Just, Rachel thought as she put one bare foot experimentally on the cold, bare floor, *as Cole and I are to one another. We cling together as only two people in love can who have had to endure long separations. But, please, God, don't let it always be this way...*

A door closed softly and the men were gone. Almost immediately, there was a light tapping at the bedroom window. Yolanda's signal!

Rachel motioned her inside. Then, splashing her face with water, she quickly pulled a comb through her hair. "I'll braid it while we have coffee," she said, motioning her friend to a chair.

"Braid it fast!" Yolanda's blue eyes were more alive than Rachel had seen them since Julius Doogan had broken her heart. "I've come to get you. I was prepared to wheedle, cajole, or get downright nasty. But I see you are *you* again."

Rachel nodded, knowing that the lump of sadness would never go away. But, having loved and lost, she was better prepared to understand—to weep with those who wept.

Yolanda gave her a searching look from blue, black-fringed eyes—eyes which smiled but no longer laughed. She, too, had been hurt. Rachel reached out and wordlessly they embraced.

"Now, get dressed! Once you drafted me. Now I am drafting you back to the classroom. Lots to plan. We've fallen heir to three Walter Scott novels and a dog-eared dictionary!"

4

To Be of One Mind

The next day was Sunday. Rachel had a strong feeling that neither Sam Blevins nor Ponce LaRue had attended church before. Aunt Em, who served them sourdough biscuits (explaining that the cows were "dry"), gravy, and some of her choice pullet eggs, told them attendance was her pay.

"Th' Frenchman looked kinda taken aback," the older woman confided later, "mutterin' somethin' about not goin' in the' Old Country less'n it be Christmas or All Souls' Day. And I up 'n told him *every* Sunday was all souls' day hereabouts."

Both of the men appeared uncomfortable. Intending to be inconspicuous, they seated themselves off to one side of the Meeting House, near the side door, as if to plan ahead for an early escape. Poor planning, they were soon to realize. The congregation filled the split-log benches from back to front, clustering to the opposite side where an ancient harpsichord stood propped against the wall, having lost one of its legs in its journey West. The instrument belonged to Yolanda's family—rightfully a treasure to the Irish

Lees. Unable to afford an education for their daughter, it was a source of pride that Nola taught Yolanda to coax something akin to music from the out-of-tune keyboard.

And so it was that, although the large congregation of "souls" sat on the right, the eyes of the souls were focused on the strangers. Because, alas, they found themselves very much on stage. What was more, Rachel—watching the men—realized that the inevitable had happened. They had attracted unwanted attention. The entire church and everyone in it seemed to be holding their breath. In a sort of chain reaction, each pair of eyes centered them out, then sent a coded message to the person across from, in back of, and in front of them.

Something is in the wind, the silent communiques read. Or, as Brother Davey would have phrased it: "Bein' likeminded, havin' one head betwixt us—"

And, typically, his wife would have prompted, "One *mind*, Davey. And th' same love, like Paul told th' Philippians."

David Galloway would take no offense. Contrary to the concerns of Cole, who saw the little itinerant (and illiterate) preacher as a member of his "family" to be cared for but allowed to maintain his dignity, Brother Davey had welcomed the more progressive young minister who was willing to divide his time between preaching here and pursuing his studies at the seminary some 200 miles away.

"What denomination?" Judson Lee's Irish brogue was exaggerated, burring his speech, so determined was he that the Word of the Lord remain strictly that in this "borrough."

It was Yolanda who calmed her father. "No denomination, Pa—just preaching."

Putty in the hands of his daughter, Judson had agreed to let the young man come. Once, mind you!

And, taking over, he had said, "Now, be ye knowin' that we're simple folks—wantin' for no changes. Best we be meetin' like the disciples did on the first day o'th' week to break th' loaf and implore th' assistance of the Heavenly Father in encouragin' one another in th' heavenly ways. Be ye o'that mind, Good Brother?"

The "Good Brother" (in reality a 24-year-old, shy-speaking youth with the down of early manhood still on his frequently blushing cheeks) dared be of no other mind. However, when he spoke, his delivery, his sincerity, and his familiarity with the Bible wiped away his shyness and the suspicions of the settlers. The text could not have been better.

> Fulfill ye my joy, that ye be like-minded, having the same love, being of one accord, of one mind. Let nothing be done through strife or vainglory; but in lowliness of mind let each esteem other better than themselves...not every man on his own ...but...on the things of others. Let this mind be in you, which was also in Christ Jesus...

Since Timothy Norvall's first visit, Brother Davey's favorite quotations had been from the book of Philippians, both in the pulpit (when Timothy was not present), and to prove a point in his frequent arguments.

Today, when the familiar chords filled the church under Yolanda's gifted fingers, the congregation seemed to sing louder than usual. Almost, Rachel thought, in supplication. She wondered what it was they expected of the two who were strangers in their midst.

Rachel felt Cole's hand reach for hers. And across

the room she encountered Buck's gray eyes on them, smiling as it were in encouragement. Something of former years was back. Back to stay. The world around her was suddenly light. Iridescent as a bubble which, it if floated away, would drift toward heaven with her, Cole, Star, and this entire congregation inside. They were indeed of one mind . . .

The bubble bounced back to earth. Judson Lee's mellow bass voice had stopped. Brother Davey was "speakin' in th' absence of my younger brother in the service o'th' Master—prepared, like always t'receive th' word straight from th' mouth o'th' Lord." He talked on about "knowin' th' Good Book by heart—bottom t' top." Then, surprisingly, he stopped. The Lord, he said, had not laid the words on his heart. There were guests who, after collection, might be wishing to speak a few words.

Rachel felt Cole shift uneasily against her. There would be—*could* be—no secrets between these people. Both she and Cole knew that. She tried to catch his eye when she accepted the hat from his hand, dropped in an offering, and passed it on to her neighbor. But Cole was looking to their right, as was everybody else. All eyes were on the two men who had wished to play down their presence— and certainly to keep their mission here secret.

She followed the glances, half hoping to see the engineer and the surveyor slide through the side door. Instead, they sat statue-still, their features set in perplexity.

Brother Davey's walk back to the crude pulpit was a near strut. Taking his time, the little man took out each bill and coin, counting and recounting, while yanking dangerously hard all the while on his side-beard. At last, he raised sad eyes to the congregation. "Not much rejoicin' in heaven today," he said. "Nothin' but widders' mites and us needin'—"

Buck saved the moment by stepping forward. "Perhaps we should postpone business for the deacons' meeting," he said pleasantly but with a note of authority. "Some of our congregation, having come 30 miles, will wish to be on their way home. But you will all be happy to know that the glass for the windows will be arriving this week."

There were cheers. Buck raised his hand for silence then continued, "In closing, Brother Davey," he said pointedly, "Let us thank the Lord that we no longer have to sleep 70 to a cabin or in a barn to keep out of the rain during a revival meeting. The Lord has provided well for us."

"Amen!" Brother Davey affirmed. "Him and Cole. Now, about our guests. . . ."

"Yes, we shall welcome them at the close of the service." Then, turning quickly to Yolanda, Buck nodded. At his signal, her fingers struck the chords of the closing hymn.

Rachel joined in the singing with a smile on her face. Buck had shushed the sometimes over-talkative Brother Davey, at least temporarily. A little thread of understanding had passed between Buck and Yolanda—very slender, but a beginning. And, she, herself, was caught up again in the bubble of happiness that came of being one with God and with the man she loved. Yes, there was plenty to smile about. . .

Until the sound of Agnes Grant's voice screeched like a raven above the hum of voices around her. "They've got a secret they're hidin'. Plain t'see as th' nose on your face! Not t'be trusted, any of 'em, if you ask me. Like as not, it's got somethin' t'do with Superstition Mountain. Things ain't never gonna be right around here—"

"Not with you around, Aggie. Now, hush and

come with me!" Aunt Em spoke to the troublesome woman almost harshly.

But Rachel knew that the seeds of suspicion were sown. The words were not lost on a group who thought with one mind...

5

An Out-of-Season Rose

In the morning Rachel was awake well before it was light. Only a few sleepy birds warned that dawn was about to pin back the curtains of night. Rachel listened with a smile curving her lips at the memory of falling asleep in her husband's arms. The sweetness of his kisses lingered. Kisses that were soft and gentle with torrents of feeling raging underneath the placid surface. Life would go on normally, those tender kisses said, but only for a little while. And so they were colored by a sense of urgency for which there were no words. Gestures were their language of love. Cole's strong fingers tracing her eyebrows. Cole's lips brushing the tip of her nose, her closed eyelids, her temples where the curls escaped. And all the while, his heart beating like a hammer beneath the ear she pressed against his chest...

It was that position which served as a painful reminder that they were not just any happily-forever-after couple. For beneath her cheek Rachel had felt something metallic, hard, and cold. She traced it with a finger. A cross!

"It's been there all along," Cole whispered against her hair.

"Before we met?"

"Yes. It belonged to my father. Something he took to sea, only he wore it on the outside of his shirt as a sort of testimonial of his faith, also an offer to minister to those in need during time of storm—"

"And you, Cole?"

"I choose to wear it close to my heart as a reminder that God is always near—and now you are there, too."

Yes, she could understand that his father in his deadly calling to the sea would feel a need to have something tangible to hang onto. But Cole? With a sinking heart, Rachel was reminded that his calling here was just as deadly. The knowledge accounted for her wearied look that concerned Buck, as well as the charged tone in her own otherwise gentle voice. Any trip to the city for business or supplies could be Cole's last. There were Indians, highwaymen, and, yes, there was still the half-beaten enemy camp, led by Julius Doogan, out there. Their leader was doing time now, but . . .

To keep from crying out, Rachel reached up with sudden urgency and pulled Cole's face down to hers.

"I wish—oh, Cole, I wish—" Tears choked her voice.

"I do, too, Rachel. And one day it will happen. I will be home for good." Cole paused, then said a little too brightly, "There's less danger than I sense you are imagining, Rachel, but I do want you to know that the cross is engraved now. It bears our initials and the date of our marriage. Sort of an identification or signal if—"

"Oh, Cole—don't! You're breaking my heart."

Cole's arms tightened. "I didn't mean to make you sad, my darling. I meant to make you happy."

She clung to him until she stopped trembling. And then she fell asleep in his arms. Now, in the first moment of awakening, it was only the feel of his arms she remembered. She reached out to recapture the moment. But it was gone. Cole had risen ahead of her.

Rachel dressed quickly and went into the kitchen just as the first faint dawn light crept through the yellow curtains. The smell of coffee blessed the air. And Cole, already buttoned into a light jacket, extended a closed fist.

"Hold out your hands and shut your eyes."

She obliged in the little game they played. And immediately she felt something cool and moist—something wrapped in a damp cloth. Slender-bodied with a round lump on one end, it felt like a miniature mummy. What on earth...?

"Careful," he cautioned, not making her guess this time. "It's a rooted slip of the Sunshine rose to match your curtains. Supposed to bloom in the spring, I think. I ordered it from Aunt Em's seed catalogue. Must've been sent by camel. I left it in my vest pocket all night, so it may be budding by now."

Rachel could not have explained her sudden tears. The little gift pleased her more than she could say—symbolizing anew that love like theirs knew no season.

Star, tugging Moreover along by his ruff and chatting away about school, joined them. Wasn't Daddy glad Mother Mine would be going back to school with her this Monday morning? Cole, looking surprised, was indeed glad. Rachel knew by the private way his eyes smiled straight into hers, widening enough to crinkle the corners with fine, dark lines, enlarging the dark irises. He would be working discreetly with the engineer and the surveyor today, she knew without being told. But his eyes said there would be tonight. Coloring under his gaze, Rachel knew there would be no need to pinch color into her cheeks today as there had been in the pale days past.

A little nervous about the day ahead, she cast a quick glance at her fragmented reflection in the mirror. The mirror zigzagged with cracks and the silver coating was peeling from the back. Might as well look at herself in a galvanized pail!

"I've ordered my mother's old-fashioned bevel-edge mirror sent from the East." Cole's words surprised and delighted her. "But while we wait," he continued, "you can use my eyes. Come closer!"

Rachel walked toward him, feeling beautiful in his eyes. Never mind that the pink checks were fading from her calico dress, the ruffles a little frayed. She had been lost in the lap of a great depression when Cole brought the bright new bolts of material to be distributed among the women of the settlement. Not caring then, Rachel had watched in detachment as the others divided the fabric. Now she wanted to be lovely again in the mirror of his eyes. Was it vain to want a new dress?

Cole caught Rachel and Star to him for one lovely moment and then he was gone. Star gave Moreover a bear hug, reminding him that he must practice barking in Spanish as well as English. Then she, too, skipped out the door—more hurriedly than usual and with a gleam in her eye.

Rachel smoothed her hair then looked around the room. Bag...lesson-plan book...Star's lunch bucket. But something seemed undone. Everything looked in place in the crowded quarters, so she opened the door and stepped into the freshness of the morning. The snow had not lingered.

That was it! The snow was out of season. All the same, the rose cutting had sought spring in the darkness. A lovely thought. One which was interrupted by a rush of footsteps behind her. Rachel knew without turning that they belonged to Star when Moreover sniffed at the door and began his all-over wagging barking.

Star held up a small dirt-filled hand. "My father brought home a miracle, but we must help it grow."

Rachel knew then what she had overlooked. It was up to God's people to nourish His miracles. A rose. Life. She and Star must pot the Sunshine rose.

Somewhere on the bottom shelf of the worktable Cole had built beneath the window there was an earthenware pot. Bending over to search for it, she was unaware that someone had entered the kitchen—except that it was quiet, *too* quiet. Star had stopped her excited chatter and Moreover had stopped barking as if suddenly throttled. Rachel's fingers closed around the cool smoothness of the pot and she rose a little uneasily.

"Cole!" Rachel almost dropped the pot in the unexpected joy of seeing him. It looked hopeless to make her way to him as he was being smothered by kisses of welcome by Star, who was pushing futilely at Moreover's bulky body.

"How is it that Moreover always gets to you first, Daddy Mine?" Star demanded indignantly.

"Because his tongue's longer!" And the two of them doubled in laughter at their joke, then opened their arms to include Rachel.

"What did you forget?" Rachel asked practically.

"What did you forget?" Cole mimicked affectionately. "This," he kissed Rachel warmly on one cheek then the other, "and *this*." He bent to kiss the top of Star's crown of raven hair. Then, feigning a sigh, "And *this*!" He ruffled the Irish wolfhound's bangs.

"*Now*, can we get down to the family business of planting our first rose?"

"Who will fill the pot with earth?" Cole asked with a straight face. Star's face, too, was sober.

" 'I will!' said the Little Red Hen. And she did."

Rachel watched the two of them act out Star's favorite bedtime story with a glow in her heart. She tiptoed away quietly as father and daughter completed the ritual of planting their miracle. One day they would transplant it to their new home.

In the pantry she was sure a last jar of wild huckleberries remained. Aunt Em had shown her that they were every bit as good as the blueberries Mother used for making pancakes. If she had the pancakes ready by the time the Sunshine rose was potted, Cole could not refuse a hearty breakfast. Quickly, she sifted the flour and mixed the batter.

Her timing was perfect. "Who shall eat the pancakes?" Rachel sang out in keeping with the spirit of the celebration.

And, sure enough, "We will!" her family sang back.

"Kind of sneaky—sneaky-wonderful!" Cole whispered against her ear as he seated her at the small table.

And then the three of them sat down, joined hands, and Cole said a beautiful prayer of thanksgiving for the family God had given him. Rachel and Star added soft *Amens*. When the three of them looked down at Moreover, his furry paws were obediently over his eyes as Star had taught him.

It was comical one moment. It was beautiful the next. And forever memorable. "*El perro* is thankful for our miracle, too," said Little Star.

6

Whispers

December 1.

Inside the classroom, the children clustered around Rachel. Warming her heart. Making her glad to be among them again. Reassuring her that God, Who has a purpose for everything, was pointing out a path of service which would help to ease the sorrow of her loss.

"Miz Rachel, Miz Rachel!" the children cried out over and over, swinging on the folds of her skirt, vying for her hand, looking up at her with adoring eyes.

Yolanda, her red hair fluffed becomingly about her face, came to Rachel's rescue. "Give her air!" she told the giggling children. "Go help Star put up the latest pictures." To Rachel she said, "The child is a genius—and the others learn so fast from her."

"And from you," Rachel said, following her friend's finger around the room to where the pictures Star drew were pasted on the rough walls of unpeeled logs. "Without you I could never have managed this squirming mass of humanity!"

"And without *you* I couldn't have been here. I am in your debt for so much, Rachel...a wonderful friend who tutored me in the arts of ciphering, morals, and manners...then tugging me here to work with you and restore my sanity—"

"As you are doing for me now," Rachel answered with a catch in her throat. "Come, come. Want the children to see us crying? The pictures *are* good, aren't they?"

"And the children thought you would enjoy the colored leaves." Yolanda seemed in a hurry to divert Rachel's attention past the portraits to the festoons of crimson and russet maple leaves the children had swung from the rafters.

Did she imagine it or was Yolanda under some kind of pressure? The pictures? Or was it something else?

Murmuring a few words she hoped were appropriate about the loveliness of the garlands of autumn leaves, Rachel walked to the wall where the pictures were mounted. Almost immediately her gaze came to rest on the face of a beautiful woman, the perfect features surrounded by clouds of raven hair. The face seemed vaguely familiar. But where...?

And then she saw the other picture. The picture which had identified Star's abductor. The man who had betrayed the wagon train and broken Yolanda's heart. "Julius Doogan," she whispered, regretting it when she saw the look of pain in Yolanda's eyes. "I'm sorry—it's over—"

But Yolanda was shaking her head. "There's something we need to talk about, but not where the children will hear—"

But at that moment, Yolanda's oldest brother, Abe, came bringing Bibles. "I gotta tell you! There's whispers 'bout gold—"

7

The Rumors Spread

So here it comes, Rachel thought, as she thanked Abe and put the Bibles away without responding to his comment. She had known from her very first meeting with Sam Blevins and Ponce LaRue that, no matter how tight-lipped they tried to be about their mission, word would get out eventually. But even Rachel had not expected it so soon. Once whispered, news would spread like wildfire throughout the compound.

Unease had lain dormant in the corner of her mind. In the joy of being able to reenter the real world with Cole at the center, Rachel had not wanted anything to spoil their togetherness. And, most of all, not a discussion of a project which would take him on new missions. Cole, she sensed, had wished that the possibility of gold veins hidden between the layers of sedimentary rock and earth whose strata formed the towering peak of Superstition Mountain be kept secret to avoid raising false hopes among the settlers.

But Abe's whisper prodded Rachel's unease to new

life. Now it must be faced. Shattering. Inevitable. The thought came to her that the quiet of the peaceful little valley, lying apart from and almost untouched by the outside world, was destined to change. This was history in the making. Nothing anybody could do now would alter it . . .

Rachel's first day back went smoothly. It was remarkable how much progress the children were showing considering that they had almost nothing with which to work. There were few pencils, no chalk or chalkboards, and the only library consisted of the Bibles Cole had smuggled along the Oregon trail in the false bottom of his wagon, and now the Scott novels and one dictionary for 100 children.

But these books were luxuries, as was the building. Their only education heretofore had been what parents could remember—transmitted by carving the ABC's on shingles split from a tree and shaved down smooth with a jackknife. From the bed of the nearby creek they had taken chunks of soft red rock, splintered off pieces, and used them for chalk with which to print. Some of the "pencils" (melted-down bullets) remained in use now. Things would be so different when the supplies Cole had ordered came.

"Doing pretty well, aren't they?—considering that neither of us is a bonafide teacher. Not that a certificate an inspired teacher makes!" Yolanda said at Rachel's elbow.

Rachel nodded absently. "It's God's work, not ours," she said—meaning it. Then her mind returned to the rumors.

"Worried about the talk?" Yolanda had read her mind.

At Yolanda's question, Rachel turned to meet her eyes. Worried? She was frantic inside. But on the outside, she was her usual composed self, the self that pioneer life as Cole's wife had shaped her to be. Forcing her voice to remain steady, she said, "I wonder where it all began."

"The talk? I blush to say that we can lay part of it at least at the door of my father," Yolanda, who could never be anything less than honest, replied. "Tell you later," she whispered as a wee girl handed her a worn hair ribbon which had come untied from her ginger braids.

"Later" was after the two girls were able at last to clear the room of eager learners. "Now," said Yolanda. And her story began.

"You know Pa—always fishing. Fortunately, he was alone that day when the swift stream carried away his lines. Searching, he found something else instead! Something he called 'yellow stone' at the roots of the grass along the bank—"

"Is that the stream that heads on top of the mountain?"

Yolanda nodded. The stone was soft, she said—so soft her pa could pound it into any shape. And would Rachel believe he pounded the metal around those "blooming fishlines"...maybe, just maybe, making himself the only man alive fishing with sinkers of *pure gold*?

"It's true then?" Rachel's words were a whisper.

"Oh, it's true all right. Pa kept his find a secret from us all, gave Cole a sinker on the sly—and you can guess the rest."

Yes. Cole would have taken the metal to have it assayed. Undoubtedly, the assayer had found in the lump a large component of gold. Hence, the surveyor and the engineer. Rachel felt a strange thrill of excitement, mixed with a certain sadness and apprehension.

"This may be the lost gold mine, real—not legendary?"

"Of course! It's called 'Blue Bucket Mine,' supposedly because a family of immigrants left two blue buckets beside the stream when—"

"When what, Yolanda?"

"There was a massacre. Superstition Mountain and the surrounding territory's hallowed to the Indians, you know—a resting place between earth and their Happy Hunting Ground. Didn't you know any of this?"

"I knew there had been a mine at one time and a cave-in—" Rachel shuddered, remembering the signs of human remains in the basin at the top, the frightening stories that the fun-loving Irishmen kept alive which furnished grist for the mill of Agnes Grant's wagging tongue. Would it all start anew?

The windowless room had grown dark. Rachel suddenly wanted to be home. She needed to talk to and be held by her husband.

But outside she was detained, frightened by what she saw. Knots of people were hovering together, eyes fixed on the mountain that cast a long shadow above the valley.

8

Amity

The dark clouds of winter had hidden the face of a pale sun. But sunbeams danced in Rachel's heart when Cole told her that he would be staying a day or so and that they could visit among the settlers.

"And just be *folks*," he smiled, drying the last of the supper dishes.

"Oh, Cole, nothing could make me happier—and they need your presence. We *all* do. We so seldom have time to just sit and enjoy one another's company the way Yolanda's mother says they did in earlier days."

"Well, my sweet," he promised, "we shall mend that."

They visited the O'Gradys and talked about the winter wheat crop. The men looked at the new barn in which they would store the grain while Rachel and Elsa whispered secrets about the O'Gradys' expected new arrival and the children played. At the Farnalls, the subject of the city came up and the four of them joined in a lively discussion. Then, of course, their visit with the Lees took an entire day.

"There be no greater reunion this side o'heaven than this, lad!" Judson boomed as they ate their way through mountains of food.

"Oh, it's so good—so wonderful to visit and fellowship with them all, Cole!" Rachel said with deep appreciation.

Cole grinned. "And me—I get to show off my family!"

It was a beautiful time together. Rachel postponed the news which she knew would come. It came the day after their visit with the Lees. But, at least, the settlers were reassured that Colby Lord and his wife *cared*. As family, they understood.

It was best, Cole pointed out to Rachel, that a small party of men pitch camp as they surveyed a wide area surrounding Superstition Mountain. It would save time and hopefully throw curiosity seekers a little off guard.

Rachel offered no objection. Since it appeared preordained that her life would be one of apartness from the man she loved, she would play her part well—at least in his presence. But Cole would never know how many, many nights that she prayed herself to sleep, awakening in the wee hours of the lonely nights to find her pillow soaked with tears shed even while she slept.

Had Cole realized, she wondered, just what he left her to reckon with? Questions increased with what the settlers termed his "strange disappearance." It had not occurred to her to wonder if Buck accompanied the party. And when he stepped abruptly into the classroom one morning, her heart filled with joy and relief. And something in his manner told her there was news, even before he held up a silencing hand to encourage all the children to listen.

It was a familiar sound. Something she had heard before. A long time ago. But where and when? Rachel strained her ears and concentrated, aware that Buck was watching her with a look of gentle amusement.

"Wheels!" she cried out suddenly. "Wagon wheels!" For there came to her ears the sound she remembered so well along the trail, the sad-sweet lullaby of the gentle rolling westward. Not since the wagon train's arrival here had she heard that sound again—hundreds of wagons, it seemed, their turning wheels bringing them ever closer.

The supply wagons had come!

Rachel and Yolanda made no effort to control the excited children. This was a moment the likes of which they had never seen. What better education than *living* the learning?

What had sounded like a hundred wagons looked like a thousand. Rachel was no more able to control her excitement than to control the curious children who were running in droves with screams of "Welcome, welcome—*hurry*!"

"I wish you could see yourself," Buck said suddenly. "Your smile easily could warm this entire landscape on a rainy day!"

Dear Buck. She reached out and touched his hand in appreciation. Then, unconsciously, her grip tightened as the wagons drew close enough for her to make out their cargos.

"What in the world...?" Rachel stared wide-eyed at the first wagon.

"Makings of cooperage. Some enterprising fellow plans to manufacture woodware, including spinning wheels—"

Before Rachel could digest that piece of news, her

eyes had spotted the load of cradles and scythes for harvesting, the plows, grinding stones, rakes, hoes, and harnesses. There were barrels and barrels of nails and enough seed, it seemed to Rachel's enlarged eyes, to plant the whole Pacific Northwest. Cole had thought of everything.

Part of the freight was unrecognizable. Some of the machinery would have to do with sawmills and gristmills. Buck pointed out an odd-looking piece of equipment which he said would be a part of the telegraph office.

"It's to be put in the side-room of the hotel—oh, there's the sign!" Rachel followed his gaze: HOSTELRY!

"Aunt Em and Brother Davey will love that," she said, torn between running to alert the Galloways and staying here to watch the parade. Another sign stood erectly alongside the hotel sign: GENERAL STORE, and in smaller print below: "Ladies' Fine Wear." Oh, how exciting! She found it impossible to move.

Completely engrossed in the scene before her, Rachel had held onto Buck's hand totally unaware. Even when she saw Yolanda's blue eyes on her, she supposed it was only because Yolanda was as fascinated with the delivery as she. Rachel waved, wondering as she did so at the troubled look in the other girl's eyes. Yolanda returned the wave distractedly.

There was no time to talk, however. The children were venturing dangerously near the mule teams. The settlers, alerted by the commotion of unfamiliar sounds, were swarming from their cabins. Aunt Em, with a smudge of flour on her nose, was wiping her large, capable hands on the Mother Hubbard apron wound about her ample middle. It was she who spotted the telltale wagon first. The wagon laden with picks, shovels, blasting powder, and all the makeshift paraphernalia needed for quickly-erected mining camps.

Any moment now the others would see it, too. But, for now, it was their moment of glory. The beginnings of a real town had arrived. Just in time for Christmas.

Rolling up their sleeves, the men began helping unload the heavy equipment. Buck directed the setting up of machinery for the gristmill. "It will need to be there by the river for water power," he said.

"What'll we do fer millstones?" Brother Davey was jumping up and down in excitement.

"There's meteoric granite everywhere to be dressed out," Buck explained as he lifted an anvil. "Irons to be forged and somewhere in this load, I'm guessing, we'll find the bolting cloth—"

"So's we can supply ourselves 'n th' pack trains goin' into Californ'y—maybe up yonder—"

Buck cut him short. "Will you unload the small fruit trees, Brother Davey?"

The little man, unabashed, darted to the wagon carrying the fragile plants. Set in small boxes of earth, the tiny trees had made it all the way from the East. Rachel, looking at them, found herself marveling at the mighty arm of God. There was no way of knowing how many of the trees had perished on that long, hard journey West. But He had seen to it that a remnant was preserved. Enough, like the people He had led into this new land, to carry out His plan.

"Mrs. Lord, I believe?" Rachel jumped when the man's faintly-familiar voice spoke at her elbow.

Spinning on her heel, she was face-to-face with one of the three men Cole had brought to the settlement when the sale of the school land had been granted by the federal government. School districts were given the right to tax themselves, she remembered. A right homesteaders questioned.

"General!" Rachel exclaimed in warm welcome. "I am sorry you failed to win the bid for Territorial Governor—and I hope you have not come to collect the taxes!"

The tall, middle-aged man in uniform smiled as he climbed from his horse and took both of Rachel's hands in his own. The largeness of General John Wilkes still astounded her. And something about the just-so crease of his uniform, the regulation-straight part of his graying hair, and the twinkle in the brown eyes brought back the credence of yesterday's dreams...when life here was just beginning...when love was new...

The General brought her back to the present. "In reverse order, no, I did not win. Let us attribute my loss to our gain—gain of coming statehood. That's the way Abraham Lincoln would have phrased it most likely. He did consider an offer to the Territorial Governorship, you know."

Rachel felt her eyes widen, at which the man smiled. "Why should he turn down the draft? Mary wanted no part of the wilderness. She lacked your spunk, my dear, and may I be so bold as to add that she lacked your loveliness?"

"Thank you, Sir," she said demurely, then teasingly, "and now about the taxes?"

General Wilkes looked sober. "Money is not easy to come by. We shall hope...but let us not get into that now."

Rachel felt herself exhale. Something told her that he knew of the talk of gold here, but the same whisper told her that he—as she—did not wish to speak of it yet.

"I do have news of interest, however! I was able

to round up books which should be helpful. Not exactly to our liking, mind you, but—"

"Anything would be welcome!" Rachel said quickly.

Then they both turned to watch as men began unloading cartons she knew immediately were books. Subjects were marked clearly on the outside: history, poetry, fiction, mathematics, navigation, astronomy, law, philosophy, and a book entitled *Common Works on Milling, Engineering, Mining, Assaying, Veterinary Practices, and Other Sciences*...

For *children*?

"I'm not sure of my competency..." Rachel's voice trailed off.

"You, my dear, are capable of anything demanded of you. The qualities of the person are the qualities of the teacher. Your husband, who is so very deft and instinctive, so very determined to succeed, must have seen the same fiber in his chosen wife—not to mention her charm!"

The General let go of her hands, lifted his hat, and bowed from the waist with a graceful, sweeping gesture. How gallant the man was. And yet, it was not his sincere compliments which caused Rachel's color to heighten. His words had brought back the haunting stream of doubts. What, she wondered, would General Wilkes think of her if he knew that her father would have sold her soul for a mass of pottage? That he had all but thrust her into a marriage with Cole in order to gather the where-with to satisfy his taste for the demon rum?

"There will be other books—" General Wilkes paused as another man joined them. "You remember U.S. Marshal Hunt..."

Before he finished the sentence, the Marshal was pumping her hand, his grip as firm and his eyes as kind as Rachel recalled. "My pleasure," he said in the quiet voice she remembered. "And this is—"

"Burt Clemmons!" boomed the gaunt-faced man in faded overalls. "I'm the one needin' no shoes. Pads on my feet bein' thick."

With a mischievous grin, the wheat farmer held out a bare foot. "Could walk on nettles, them feet," he claimed. Rachel found his simplicity as touching as at their first acquaintance. Her husband, she realized anew, looked on the worth of men—not the price tags of the garments they wore.

Buck joined the foursome just as Rachel was ready to say how happy Cole would be to see them. He shook hands with the men, then turned to Rachel. "Yolanda's spotted the makings for a millinery shop," he smiled. "Maybe we've lost a teacher!"

"If you gentlemen will excuse me, I will try to rescue her," Rachel said with a laugh. *Imagine—a millinery shop!*

"Now, don't be hurryin'," Burt Clemmons said quickly. "Best Miz Lord here be knowin' 'bout the school and then the diggings—"

"Oh, the school, yes!" General Wilkes' voice was a wee bit too clipped, Rachel thought. Any mention of a possible gold strike—and there had been several near-misses—seemed to put a restraint on him. She could see his back straighten, his manner become more that of a military man.

"You see, Rachel," he said, turning to her with a sudden smile, "your school here now has a name."

Brother Davey, having finished unloading the seedlings, was running to greet the men. Above a male-voice choir of greetings, Rachel was barely able to discern the General's words: "Territorial legislature's named this the first *public* school—having dillydallied long enough over the site—*Amity*."

Amity, meaning peace. *Please, Lord, for us all,* Rachel prayed.

9

"Pandora's Box"

People gathered like a bouquet of wild flowers from the countryside. Whether they heard the wagons with the trained ear of the pioneer was moot. Rachel felt that those from surrounding areas sensed they were needed. And they were there. Instinctively, and without words, the men seemed to know where everything belonged while the women twittered in small knots "oh-ing" and "ah-ing." All except Aunt Em. In her usual no-nonsense manner, she had set up housekeeping, so to speak, in the large building now identified by the sign: HOSTELRY.

"Men'll be hungry shortly," she whispered to Rachel. "Best I be recruitin' some help. With their hands busy, maybe their tongues can rest a spell— get 'em out from underfoot, too. So," Aunt Em dropped her voice even lower, "you pick up all th' news for me, dearie. *Yoo hoo*, ladies! Right this way—"

Rachel saw that Buck was helping Yolanda gather the children together and herd them back into the

Meeting House. Not that they could concentrate. But then, who could? Smiling, Rachel moved to join them. "Amity," she would tell them, "Amity meaning peace...our first public school, the others having been missions...." What a history lesson!

But sight of another wagon caught her eye, bringing a swift end to her lesson planning. The crates in it were enormous. And over them was draped worn canvas in humps and bumps that looked like exhausted ghosts. Fascinated, Rachel took a step toward the wagon, only to feel a restraining hand on her arm.

"These, my dear, are forbidden boxes, I am afraid. Orders of your husband." The voice was that of General Wilkes.

"But I—" Rachel paused, not sure what she was about to say. Something about "Pandora's Box" maybe?

"Tut, tut, dear Rachel. Have patience. He will be home soon. That will be the proper time for the two of you to delve into personal belongings."

Rachel joined Yolanda, but her mind was elsewhere. How did the General know that Cole would be coming home soon? And what on earth was in those mysterious crates? But, intriguing as the question was, invariably her thoughts returned to Cole. *Cole is coming home*, her heart sang. *Cole is...*

But the song in her heart stopped in mid-measure. Outside there was a commotion. Excited voices said the men had discovered a Pandora's Box of their own. "Minin' gear...gold!"

10

Adam's Rib

General Wilkes, Marshal Hunt, and Burt Clemmons filled in the missing pieces one evening. It was Buck's suggestion that Rachel have them for coffee to afford a bit of privacy. Over a second cup, the General announced matter-of-factly that they had come ahead of the supply wagons and gone to the camp where Cole was working with the surveyors. Rachel wanted to hear more. But, suddenly afraid, she was silent.

She was glad when Buck posed the questions churning inside herself. "Just what are the chances up there, Sir?"

"Excellent, wouldn't you say, gentlemen?"

"Better than that!" Burt declared, draining his cup and extending it to Rachel for a refill. She obliged, listening.

"The fact that the grass grows greener on the other side of the mountain seems to be a reality on Superstition Mountain," Marshal Hunt said quietly.

The other two men nodded. And then they told their story. Cole had taken the mules to the other side for rest—and did Rachel and Buck know the snow was only partially melted and was watering a valley below—unsettled, mind you?

Rachel held her breath. "Did they—did we—?"

"Stake a claim? Oh, that we did—" General Wilkes began. And then the three men were talking at once again.

The best Rachel could make of the story was that nobody had risked offending the Indians' "hallowed ground" (although they had no claim on it, the men said). And—*Ahem!*—it seemed that most folks didn't take a shine to, well, offending the so-called "spirits" on Superstition Mountain. Not that *they* believed such. Most likely, it was unsettled because the mountain formed such a barrier.

But the gold. What about the gold?

Oh, yes, the gold! Well, the mules grew fat on the rich grass. It grew so high that a man had to stand on the back of a mule to see over it! And then one day (all voices dropped several octaves) Cole followed up a gulch where the rains had washed the earth away. He began digging on a ledge of rock with his bowie knife, and he dug out nuggets of gold. Pure gold! Already assayed. And, yes, he staked the claims properly. But the problem was that within a year thousands would be rushing in, staking claims, ravishing the rich farmlands, polluting the streams and the young women!

Rachel shuddered. But the gravity of the situation, frightening though it was, could not tarnish the shimmer of anticipation of Cole's homecoming. And besides, he would know what to do . . .

"The problem lies in deciding exactly how much to tell the others here. Most of them suspect—and suspecting can be more damaging than the truth," Marshal Hunt said after a pause.

"Not until Cole is back!" Buck's voice was firm.

"You are right, of course," General Wilkes agreed. Then, with a flourish, he removed a heavy gold watch from his vest pocket, snapped open the lid, and said, "My, my! I am afraid we have taxed your patience, Rachel, my dear. It is past midnight." Rising, he tucked the watch back into its hiding place. "My father's, and an object of pride. It is my dream that every man in this settlement should own such a treasure. Gold, it is a beautiful dream. . . ."

Unless one makes it into an idol. Rachel opened her mouth then closed it. The General was moving toward the door, hat in hand. The other two men were following.

At the door, General Wilkes paused. Turning unexpectedly, he came back to the table and picked up another molasses cookie. "You know, my dear, I must repeat an earlier statement. You are more like another Mary—Mary, the sister of Lazarus. As a matter of fact, you are patterned from both his sisters: a listener like Mary—'the good part,' I believe Jesus called it—and Martha, the worker. No, you most definitely are *not* a Mary Todd!"

Even after the men were gone, Buck lingered. It was as if he had something that needed saying and was unable to find a starting point. A creak of the door leading to the side room and the sudden appearance of Star's head peeking through the crack, dark eyes widened by curiosity, gave him an excuse for remaining.

"Star and I haven't had a cookie!" he said, making his voice very small. With a bound the child was in his arms and being swung almost to the rafters, bare brown toes wriggling with delight below her flannel nightie.

Rachel warmed the coffee and poured milk for Star.

"Thank you for all you said and did not say

tonight, Buck," Rachel said, sitting down to join them. "You really are very nice."

"Yes, I suppose I am." The words were supposed to be spoken in jest. But something in them said disappointment. Buck had folded away memories of the one love in his life, but she sensed that, even so, he was unable to get on with another love. "I'm sorry," she said without intending to.

Buck searched her face then gave her a lopsided grin.

"Don't be. I was here because I wanted to be. You needed me."

Something in his voice reached out to Rachel, caused sudden tears to gather in her eyes. On an impulse, foreign to her nature, she reached across the short span between them and brushed his cheek with a kiss. Buck smiled self-consciously.

"Lucky guy, Colby Lord—having a wife like you," he said.

"Lucky us—having a friend like you!" Rachel's words were laced with tears.

• • •

It was several days before Rachel could get around to doing something born of General Wilkes' contrasting her with the wife of Abraham Lincoln. Maybe it was vain of her to take his comments seriously, she would scold. But the niggling curiosity remained. One day, given a moment, she would check.

The settlement was swarming with unfamiliar faces now, people who were to be the shopkeepers, Buck explained. Brother Davey complained that it "itched th' brain" to see how all "them trappin's is a-gonna fit in th' space afforded." Agnes Grant stalked sulkily from one building to another, telling everybody who would listen that the "signs" were all around them—evil signs, portending disaster. Impossible for a rich man to be gettin' into heaven ...evil, all this progress...

Rachel, feeling elated one moment and drained the next, put on a fixed smile and found solace in prayer. Even the glow she had felt in anticipation of Cole's return was fading, leaving some troubling questions in its wake. It was an effort to carry on for the children.

The new books had helped, difficult in subject matter as they were, Rachel thought with satisfaction as she put away a stack of essays she had graded. Star was asleep. And, tired as her eyes were, the moment seemed right to do her private research. "Lincoln, Mary Todd," she said aloud, feeling a sort of unexplained excitement as she thumbed through her almanac. What was this? "High-spirited," the book said of Mary, "and quick-tempered. Excellent education...cultured upbringing. And, notwithstanding her vanity, ambition, and unstable temperament and"—surprise!—"Mr. Lincoln's careless ways and alternating moods of hilarity and dejection, the Lincoln marriage had turned out to be 'generally happy.' "

Generally happy? *I want more than that,* Rachel's heart cried out as she turned the wick of the oil-burning lamp low and, shielding the chimney with her hand, puffed out the blaze. The General was right. She was not a Mary Todd. But she could identify with the woman's irritation at the Lincolns' frequent periods of separation. But not coming here to be with her husband? That was unthinkable. Just ask Aunt Em. She would follow Brother Davey to the ends of the earth. And the same applied to Nola and Judson Lee. Different in temperament as they all were, they managed to be—well, she thought sleepily—"generally happy." All of them went through separations, too. She wondered if the surveyors were married. General Wilkes' had spoken of losing his "dear wife," but what about the Marshal? And was the eccentric Burt Clemmons married? Yolanda and Buck had nobody...

Rachel roused herself enough to whisper in the darkness, "Am I selfish to ask more, Lord? I took my vows to You so seriously. Cole and I are one flesh...and until death do we part...so shouldn't it be that we do not part until one of us lays the other in Your arms? Make me a Mary-Martha, Lord, not a Mary Todd. And—please—send—Cole—to—me—"

• • •

Her prayer was answered sooner than expected. Rachel was bending over, thinning the purple-topped turnips in the handkerchief-size garden behind her quarters, when there were soft footsteps behind her. At first she thought it was Star and Moreover taking turns chasing one another. Already they had trampled down the onion bed.

Then suddenly all was quiet. Too quiet. Placing a supporting hand to her aching back, Rachel straightened. And there behind her stood a bearded stranger. But where was Moreover? Why hadn't the dog barked? Something was happening inside her. Fear? No...something else—something which caused the earth to tilt crazily and three faces to blur into one. The dog, usually so protective, had leaped to the stranger's side and, with many a whimper, was licking his free hand. The other hand, she saw in that split second before full recognition came, was lifted to the bearded face—one silencing finger touching his lips. And Star, the elusive one—made more so by Rachel's constant warnings to stay clear of strangers—had lifted a finger to her own lips in response.

They—why, they were conspiring—

Cole! Something inside her—frozen for the past weeks—thawed, bringing a flood of tears. Rachel wanted to cry out a welcome, to tell him she was unable to believe he was home, that she loved him with all her heart and would never let him out of her sight again. But little gasping sobs kept getting in the way of words and she was unable to speak.

"Oh, Cole, Cole—*Cole!*" she was able to sob at last.

"Don't cry, my darling. Don't cry. I'm home—and there's news—"

"I don't *care* about news. I care about *you.*"

"I know—I know—" Cole was whispering against her hair while trying to hug Star who was gripping his legs and stroke Moreover whose whimpers had become more like howls.

The reality of being near him was even sweeter than her memories, her dreams, her fantasies. Through her tears, Rachel saw that he was thinner. And weren't there lines around his eyes which had not been there before? He had been gone only three weeks, but it seemed more like three years.

"Your memories were what kept me warm, Cole. At night I played a silly little game that you were there beside me—"

To save her life Rachel could not have avoided the stupid hiccup! But the reward was Cole's rich, beloved laugh. And somehow he had disentangled himself and was holding her and Star closer, closer, *closer* until she could scarcely breathe.

"Memories of you did more than that for me," he whispered huskily. "They kept me alive. Oh, Rachel, that you could love a dirty, ragged straggler the pressures of the weeks have made of me—you, my Adam's rib." Not a Mary. *Adam's rib!*

Her answer was to stand on tiptoe and meet his lips, feeling the salt of his tears blend with her own. The old spark was there. The spark which burst into a conflagration, making the reunion all she had dreamed . . .

Supper was a festive occasion. Cole sliced the ham, but when he offer to help further with the meal, Rachel shook her head. "It's a surprise," she said.

"I love surprises," he said. "Speaking of which—" He wiped the butcher knife and replaced it on the chopping block he had cut from the heart of an oak headed to the mill.

"Yes, speaking of which—" Rachel raised her face, rosy-cheeked from adding stovewood to the fire. "Your daughter and I are mighty curious—"

"About the mystery boxes, Daddy Mine! Must we wait?" Star's dark eyes shone with eagerness. It was unlike her to tease. But the child had never had such temptations spread before her. Rachel wondered fleetingly again where the miracle child came from. Then she dismissed the question. It was enough that God had seen fit to entrust her to their care. Watching her and Cole together warmed her heart more than the flames now hungrily gobbling the fir wood. She turned the damper down and slipped the candied yams and fat apple pie into the oven.

As she set the sourdough biscuits to rise, she listened to the game Cole was playing with Star. Cole was drawing dots across a sheet of paper. Dots which Star was to trace.

"And that, sweetheart, will give you the shape of some of the mysterious things."

"I give up," Star said at last. "You're teasing me, aren't you, my father?"

"Yes," he admitted. And together they laughed. Rachel decided to ask no more questions. Nothing mattered except the joy of her role as "Adam's rib!"

11

The Unveiling

"Aren't you even a wee bit curious about the mysterious crates?" Cole tilted his head toward the three unloaded wagons when breakfast was finished the next morning.

Curious! Rachel's heart was bursting with curiosity. "I could hardly wait for you to get yourself shaved and rested," she admitted. "That came first—"

"*First?*" he teased, causing Rachel to rush to him and snuggle against the warmth of his chest. He knew very well that neither the mysterious cargo nor his grooming came close to comparing with the incomparable joy of their togetherness. "But *now?*" She nodded without raising telltale eyes.

Star, looking for the world like a tiny, suntanned angel, was jumping up and down. "*Ahora, ahora!* Now!"

Cole smiled. "There will be no problem in getting Amity School accredited. I'll wager we're the only school around boasting near-mastery of *three* languages—English, Latin, and Spanish—thanks to my ingenious wife and my gremlin daughter." Cole tickled Star's thin little ribs, causing her to squeal with delight.

"I had Brother Davey move the wagons to the back so as to avoid some prying eyes," Cole explained as the three of them latched the door and walked in the westward direction Cole pointed.

"First, do you both want to take a guess at what I've brought you?"

"No, *no*. Let us not stall, Daddy Mine. *Por favor!*"

"Please," Rachel translated. "And I second it."

"Well, there's this." *This* was an enormous trunk, too heavy to lift from its resting place, but Cole had climbed aboard the wagon and was fitting the key into the locks.

What Rachel and Star saw rendered them completely speechless. Star's eyes, looking much too large for the childish face, were back lighted by a million candles as Cole held up a little girl's mull hat, the fluted brim trimmed with whispering pink silk ribbons to tie beneath her chin. And then a lace poke bonnet that would make her look like an adorable valentine.

"And then a fancy cord coat, a reefer with a sailor collar...pinafores...skirts. I sound like a peddler, don't I? And my little customer isn't listening!"

Star raised a grave face, her eyes meeting Cole's in solemnity.

"It is not that I do not listen. It is that I have not heard you tell of a gift for another. And she has prayed for you often. Have you brought nothing for Mother Mine?"

"I thought I remembered how wonderful you were, but I guess I didn't," Cole said in a choked voice that spoke of tears. His strong fingers combed through the child's dark hair tenderly. Tears gathered in Rachel's throat as she watched the two of them. *I have my gift*, her heart cried out when she could find no voice. *God gave me the most wonderful husband and daughter any woman ever had!*

But neither Cole nor Star would have settled for that. Cole was lifting one section of the enormous trunk and ripping away tissues, which—if witnessed by Madame Bissette, who had wrapped the packages with a near-reverence—would have caused the French woman to tear away the "rats" securing her pompadour in place. "Pleeze now you will be most careful, *Monsieur—oui?*"

"*These*, this, and *this*—for starters!" Cole now held a pair of stylish high-top shoes of white vici kid with shiny black-tipped toes. Then, to Rachel's astonished eyes, there was a plum-colored velvet dress trimmed in ecru lace . . . an elegant Coque and Maribo feather fan . . . combs . . . gloves . . . a lizard bag . . .

Star was hugging them both, murmuring words of endearment in her native tongue. And Moreover, suddenly aware of the celebration, alerted the entire village with a series of wild barks.

And so it was that the Lords were surrounded by friends at the unveiling. Disappointed at first, Rachel realized later that it was good that they had shared in her joy.

Without invitation, Brother Davey leaped aboard the closest of the three wagons. Cole turned palms up in mock despair, bringing a ripple of affectionate laughter from the onlookers, then motioned for Buck. The three men began unwinding the coverings, with Brother Davey managing to get himself tangled in the canvas sheeting time and time again. More laughter. A few teasing jeers. Then quiet.

The day had begun cloudy, predicting the unpredictable weather-wise, the month of December being such a teaser in the Oregon Country. But now fingers of sunlight probed the cloud covering, hunted out the group, and lingered. The brightness seemed to symbolize the mood of the spectators. For a moment, their questions, suspicions, fears, and hopes gave way to the excitement around them.

When Cole and Buck raised the first piece for inspection, the crowd surged forward with such force that Rachel found herself unable to see. But above the din of voices she could hear Cole explaining: "This will be the front door to the Lord home, and the latchstring will always be out! As a matter of fact, my family and I will insist that you accept our hospitality. Our house will love company! But, there's more. You see, the materials we put into it will serve to give you ideas as to what we can, and *will* provide—"

"Th' Lord willin' and if the creek don't rise!" Brother Davey interrupted with a mischievous grin.

"Well spoken," Cole smiled. "The Lord willing, our mill can hope to turn out for you the kinds of things displayed."

"If I owned a door like that one, I wouldn't care whether there was a house behind it!" Yolanda spoke at Rachel's elbow. "But why on earth are you back here? Oh, Rachel, look! They're holding it higher!"

Rachel edged her way ahead, stood on tiptoe, and managed to catch a glimpse of the most beautiful door she had ever seen. Pure oak, wasn't it? And so highly glazed she was almost certain she could see the hills reflected in the polished wood surface. And the glass...oh, the beautiful oval glass! Was that real lace in the design or the etching of some gifted fingers? Then began a parade of other items.

Her eyes caught sight of samples of mouldings for thresholds, stair rail and balusters...arch grilles...and then she was pushed aside again.

"I ain't never seen nothin' like it. My husband ain't gonna be able to promise such to his family." There was sadness in Opal Sanders' voice.

"Well, now, we ain't never had such opportunities maybe—or haven't you heard—"

There was a jostle of elbows and the rest of Elsa O'Grady's words were drowned out as Rachel was pushed forward. She wondered fleetingly where Star could be without being crushed. Then, the crowd—like the clouds—parted, just in time for her to see Star climbing aboard with her usual agility.

The rest of the unveiling was like a dream to Rachel. It was Yolanda's strong arm which propelled her to the sidelines where she could get a better view. Not that she could believe what she saw.

There was a water pump and an enormous wood range—so massive it had to be turned sideways to fit onto the bed of the wagon. "With a reservoir, folks—'n a warmin' closet, a giant six-holer—" Brother Davey began.

Aunt Em rushed to her husband's rescue. "Them's called *eyes*, Davey love," she whispered.

With a look of amusement, Buck handed the poker to Brother Davey. Cole turned then and, with a smile at Aunt Em, announced: "This six-eyed range belongs to you two, since it is a part of the hotel."

Aunt Em wiped her eyes with the corner of her apron. Brother Davey yanked at his side-beard. "Now, brethren, you know that 'Where there is no wood the fire goeth out' according to the Psalms—"

"Proverbs, Davey," Aunt Em said, handing him the axe.

Even above the laughter came the cries of delight when Cole and Buck rapidly lifted the canvas from a tall chifforobe with a golden finish...a washstand with serpentine posts for a mirror...a rolltop desk...a poppy-painted lamp...and a magnificent brocaded velour Empress-design couch. These? For *her*?

"Oh, Yolanda," she breathed. "Is it really true?"

Yolanda was misty-eyed. And there was a note of sadness in her voice. "True, Rachel. How blest you are."

Yes, Cole had unveiled his heart.

12

A Time To Dance

Rachel still stood with a dream in her eyes when suddenly she realized that she was in the grip of two powerful arms. "Isn't it time you joined your husband?"

Cole! "But the people—the others—" Rachel spoke foolishly as if awakened too soon.

"It's all right. They've heard the rumor that we're married!" And with the warmth of his soft, rich laugh still on her cheeks, Rachel allowed herself to be escorted to the last of the three wagons. Buck was waiting with an extended hand. And suddenly the interrupted dream began anew. This couldn't be happening. Her mother's china cabinet...

Feebly, she reached out to touch it to make sure. Humbly, she stroked the warm surface of the age-smoothed wood, felt the familiar coolness of the thick bent glass ends and the front of the five-shelved cabinet. In it Mother had kept Rachel's dolls, her baby shoes, the family Bible, and a hand-painted set of robin-egg-blue china dishes. The mirrored back was still intact, causing a lump to rise in her throat at memory of her favorite childhood game. When Mother's illness became too much for a little girl's heart, Rachel would steal away to sit before the cabinet, gazing into the mirror, and seeing reflected there two of everything she held dear. She created a lovely fantasy. In it she could enter the other world through the looking glass anytime. As she was doing now!

"Oh, Cole," she whispered, "how did you get it here from the East?" But she was too overcome to hear his reply.

Besides, Star was calling in excitement. "Mother Mine, *madre mia! Es muy bonita*—very beau-ti-ful!"

Muy bonita indeed! Buck has stripped the wrappings from a splendid brass bed, the heavily ornamented knobs atop each post capturing the light to form an earthbound galaxy. The crowd was pushing forward again in an effort to get a better view. Some applauded. Others wept. Rachel realized then that it was Cole's words that moved them—Cole's explaining that the bed had belonged to his parents . . . an heirloom . . . and that his mother's cheval mirror for the washstand was on its way.

Then a thunderbolt struck. The raucous voice of Agnes Grant cut the world in half. "Solid gold, I betcha. Gold from that evil place. Only he ain't tellin' what we rightfully oughta be knowin'—lest we all perish. Gold, I tell you—"

Her words were smothered by Aunt Em's capable hand. "Cease fire, Aggie! Evil words are worse'n bullets." And she pulled the hysterical woman away.

But the peace of the day was shattered. General John Wilkes was the first to realize it. Shoulders squared, he marched briskly to where Cole, Buck, and Brother Davey were unwrapping what appeared to be school supplies and several hymnals.

A few words later, the four men called Marshal Hunt, the surveyors, and the Council. Even as they talked briefly, there arose a murmur. The murmur swelled, turning to hoots, jeers, and whistles of impatience. The glory of the curtain-raising day had turned to suspicion, too long withheld. Rachel looked about anxiously. *Please, Lord, no division...*

The General's military training gave command to his voice. "Tonight we men shall gather at the Meeting House. There are announcements and a need for planning." His face lost a bit of its grimness as he looked directly at Rachel. "Perhaps, Mrs. Lord, you and the other ladies will join us at the hotel later. It is entirely possible that we shall find this requires a celebration—shall we say, a time to dance?"

• • •

For Rachel the minutes dragged into hours, making a long waiting period in spite of her busy hands. Feeling that the men would need support, she had passed along the word that punch and pound cake would be nice. Coffee? Yes. And why not make it special for the men by dressing? A suggestion welcomed by the women as each went her separate way.

Now, they were back together. Tasting the punch which had been declared just right hours before. Rearranging the buttery slices of cake. And frequently looking out the windows to where moonlight glinted off the polished windows of the Meeting House in response. Waiting for their husbands, they were silent.

Rachel busied her hands with arranging an armful of wild sumac in an earthenware pot. What would they be saying—the men? Cole would be announcing his finds. Now, Ponce would explain his geological sightings. Positive, he'd declare. Moving one of the red-berried branches toward the center, Rachel went on with her countdown. Buck, discussing city finances. General Wilkes, warning of the need for added defense. The Council—she counted them off on her fingers beneath the winter bouquet—would speak in turn regarding the safety of the children. She hoped they would pray together, maybe sing.

Frowning a little, Rachel removed the last cluster of the bright branches. Maybe the bouquet was overloaded. Biting on the stem, she thought back to something about General Wilkes' behavior that bothered her. Beneath the military-man exterior there was something watchful, guarded, even uneasy. He, of all people in the settlement, knew the meaning of bloodshed—brother against brother being more tragic than declared war. She dropped the thought and turned to the other women as there was the sound of men's voices. The meeting was over!

"It went well," Yolanda broke the silence with a laugh. "Listen to my father!" Judson Lee's voice was bouncing against the canyon walls, a happy seafaring song, that broke the tension and let the women burst into needed laughter.

Yolanda picked up the spray of wild holly berries Rachel had discarded, broke off a twig, and tucked it into her upswept auburn hair. Catching Rachel's eye, she colored.

"Well," she said defensively, "they match my blouse."

Rachel noticed then that Yolanda wore a sheer red top, laced with a black velvet ribbon at the neck. For whom?

"Not that I look like you, of course." Yolanda's voice carried a blend of admiration and melancholy

—something that only time or the right man could erase.

Remembering her vow not to interfere, Rachel concentrated on her own dress, smoothing the folds of the wild-rose silk, unaware that its soft color reflected in her cheeks. She had chosen it simply because it was on top of the stack of clothes Cole had brought and would need no pressing.

"Now," she asked anxiously, "Do I look over-dressed? It's a simple dress, but is it all right—I mean am *I*?"

"I don't know *what* you mean. But you look like a wood nymph."

By then the men had burst into the dining room with all the noise and exhilaration that Rachel remembered hearing from a distance at the local pubs near her eastern home. All were talking at once, and Rachel knew immediately that the gaiety of the day had come back, then multiplied tenfold.

General Wilkes was right in his concerns. Ahead lay the probability of countless dangers. But for now those dangers were something they would cope with later. Rachel was wrestling with problems of her own. If, as these men were expecting, there was enough gold to warrant mining on a large scale, would this mean more separations for her and Cole?

Then she, too, cast her worries aside. She had caught sight of Cole making his way toward her. His eyes were shining with victory. But when his gaze locked with hers, there was a new light. The unmistakable shine of love!

Forgetting formality, Rachel lifted her long skirt and ran, meeting Cole halfway in the center of the room (or was it the universe?), his hands holding hers. And then his arms were around her. Like Cole said, she thought dreamily, their friends knew they were married! Smiling at the thought, she pressed her cheek to his, knowing that they held something between them that was warm and wonderful. Something very rare. Something very sacred that God had used to bring them together. She felt as if she were floating to heaven to thank Him.

She was glad for the sudden wail of a fiddle. Glad for the sudden whirling of skirts as the men's long-stemmed legs, so used to hard work, now tapped out "Turkey in the Straw." And glad that the children had formed a circle and were engaging in a happy game of their own. Glad, because their happy activity gave her an opportunity to be "alone" with Cole, even in a crowd. Oh, the God-given gladness of it all!

For a moment they did not speak. They just "belonged." Everything was so right and so beautiful. His strong hand supporting her back. Throbbing through the sheer wild-rose-colored bodice possessively. And Rachel yielding...

It was she who broke the silence. But the spell lingered.

"It went well, didn't it. And you believe—"

"The meeting went well indeed," Cole said against her hair. "And what I believe is that the hand of God will guide us toward progress such as I never dreamed. I furthermore believe—no, I *know*—that we will live happily forever after!"

His words made her want to cry. But this was not a time to weep. It was a time to be happy—only—

"Did I choose the right dress from those you bought?"

"You look beautiful, little Bunny Face." Cole held her closer, his use of the affectionate name he'd created on the trail causing a lump in her throat.

"What's bothering you, darling?" Cole's question surprised her. But then she was transparent where he was concerned. There was no use holding back.

76

"Cole, will all this make a difference—take you away?" *Oh, please, Lord, no,* her heart implored. *At least not far. Or for long.*

"It is hard to say. But this I can promise: not for a long, long time. We have our *now.* Can we ask more of the Lord?"

Everyone around them seemed to be beaming, as if happy just for them. Dreaming, yet wide awake, Rachel's heels took wing. "A time to dance . . ." How beautiful were the words!

13

Peace in the Valley

There followed a time of peace in the valley—and in Rachel's heart. The future lay ahead: bright, shining, and as reassuring as the flashing stone in her wedding ring.

By almost superhuman endeavor and courage the settlers had achieved their first goal. A few cabins were dotting the cleared fields like daisies. Soon building of the new school would begin. And there would be a church—in accordance with Judson Lee's "non-denominational" dream.

Soon hills would grow green. Flocks of sheep and herds of cattle would graze the sumptuous pastures. Brooks—usually dry as spring gave way to summer —would dance full this year, and barns were sure to bulge with bountiful harvest. So Rachel dreamed on and drank from the beauty of the Lord's loving cup, marveling at the serenity of the settlers. Why not? These wonderful people, so faith-filled and dedicated to the will of their Father, could bury their dead with stern fortitude and move on in spite of their sadness, looking forward to another turn of the seasons, a wedding, a birth, and now a new adventure! "Yellow Metal Days," they called it. At first, the men had been impatient with the delay. Equipment was here. They were ready. But Cole would not be coerced or hurried. Digging would begin when he had protected every family in the settlement. Proper papers were being processed in which each homesteader within the parameter the church and school served would be a shareholder. Grumbling halted. The men were speechless in their unbelievable good fortune.

But how, Rachel wondered, could these sturdy people fail to foresee what lay between the burying of the past and the unearthing of the future? Below the surface of her own bubbling happiness she felt a sort of melancholy, a fear of change that was inevitable. A fear of the end of the lovely peace.

"Pray without ceasing" became her biblical motto. There was a constant prayer on her lips—mostly petitioning the Lord to forgive her misgivings. "I know my words are jumbled, Lord," she said on one particular morning. "How can I ask that You bring prosperity to these deserving people while begging that things can remain the same for Cole and me? But You have made us one, Lord. Don't let gold put asunder what You have brought together. Lord, just *understand* me. . . ."

Rachel tried to assuage her concern with domestic zeal. She collected recipes from Aunt Em to Star's delight. But, largely, Cole left her apple turnovers and cherry cobblers untouched. He looked tired— so tired. She wished he would share his concerns but did not push him. She met him each day with a serene face, a brilliant smile, and what the two of them still shared when the day was done. "Honeymoon eyes, honeymoon eyes that could see love in the dark. . . ."

She cleaned the cabin until it shone. She unpacked, pressed, and put away the lovely wardrobe Cole had brought for her and Star. She did her hair a new way with wispy bangs across her round forehead. They added delicacy, Rachel thought, to her strongly-marked brows. Of course, they would be curling uncontrollably by the time Cole came home.

Cole was forever attending one of his meetings. Soon they would be ending, he told her. Papers almost in order. Promise of a ship tying up in the inlet of the river. Yes, this way, the gold—should there be a sizable strike—could be transported quietly to Portland. Less danger than trying to take the inland route. The words frightened Rachel. So she cleaned more. Baked more. Dreamed up new projects for the classroom. And prayed. And all the while prayed.

"Let things stay the same while they change, Lord—if You can work it into Your plans..."

And then she saw the signs of an increasing intensity among the men who were working closest with Cole. But there was a comforting closeness about them, too. There was something she could only describe as a "razor look," a sharpness in their eyes even when their mouths were stretched into smiles. Shouldn't they invite the men to the cabin? Rachel's suggestion caused Cole to hold her close, his hand twisting at the wispy bangs. Maybe talking things out would help.

"Have you any idea how wonderful you are? How much I love you? What all I want to do for you?" he asked huskily.

The lump in Rachel's throat choked off the words. *Oh, my darling, I don't want anything for myself except what you have given me, the wonderful world of your love!*

From somewhere in a far corner of her mind she

heard Cole say it would be wonderful, yes, to wind up the business in their temporary home. And so it was that the General, the Marshal, Burt Clemmons, Ponce, Sam, and the Council made the cabin their headquarters. Then, of course, there was Brother Davey, dear Brother Davey, always so vocal and so visible. And Buck. Buck was there most of all. Devouring her muffins, cornbread sticks, and sourdough pancakes after church on Sunday. He was Cole's right arm. He was Star's playmate. He was Rachel's shoulder to cry on when she hid her tears from Cole. Buck was family.

The men, Rachel thought, as she dished up black-berry dumplings, looked like large cardboard cutouts—grim, stiff, lips curved in unmoving smiles—the night they declared the way was cleared for mining to begin.

Brother Davey broke the tension by saying, " 'Course now, we won't be allowin' th'heart t'know what the head's doin'!"

Aunt Em, entering to bring cream for the dump-lings, smiled. "The Good Book says it another way, Davey love—it's th' right hand not knowin' 'bout th' left!"

But the "right hand" knew what the "left" was doing as far as neighboring was concerned. During Cole's time at home, he had seen to that.

"There's so much I can lend a hand on that has nothing to do with the mine or the city," Cole said. "Let's be sure we squeeze in a margin of time for helping get the cabins as nearly completed as possible—and," he smiled, "that means visiting time for you ladies!"

"*Visiting* time!" Rachel pretended to be shocked. "Fat chance—as much as you men eat. Oh, Cole, you know I'd love that—the talking, the building, the being together!"

"You know, I sure got myself some wife," Cole said, with an affectionate pinch of her cheek.

"And, you know, I sure got myself some fellow!" Rachel tweaked him on the nose just as Star and Moreover came bounding in to know what they were whispering about.

"Secrets," Cole said mysteriously, then shared the plans. "And, of course, we will need one small girl and one big dog."

So, as a happy family, the young Lords went wherever they were needed. By mutual consent, the settlers decided that work went faster—" 'n shure a whole lot pleasanter"—if they worked together. Rachel was right. The men were a hungry lot. She was right, too, about the fun of such work days. The men, women, and children clung to these days, stretching them out as one holds onto a fading summer. Reminiscent of days on the trail, they built campfires at night around which the children danced and the grownups talked until well past midnight—nobody seemed to mind...

14

"A Cup of Gold"

There had been little snow and spring came early. By February the hills were painted with yellow buttercups and in March the radishes and red-leaf lettuce were ready for the table. April blustered in and out while ears were atuned more to the news than to the wind. Would the clouds of political differences clear? Already, Congress had passed an act cutting off the Washington Territory from the Oregon Territory. Now, Oregon stood on the doorstep of statehood. But people in the settlement were less excited over the possibility of electing their own governor (and taxing *themselves*) than the other question. "Gold in them thar hills!" became their password.

June tiptoed in softly, bringing roses and bright, moonlit nights. One by one the shops were opening. But Rachel took little notice—concentrating instead on sending silent love messages to Cole with her eyes when he seemed too preoccupied to talk. But he was never too busy to respond. His eyes sent back the messages like homing pigeons. And more. That no matter how busy the days, there were their nights.

So Rachel counted her blessings—not the falling stars of her loneliness as the town demanded more and more of Cole, but the stars that stayed intact in the brilliant sky of their moments of togetherness. Moments which could not last forever. It was not a matter of whether they must part again. It was a matter of when.

July was hot and sultry. Gardens drooped. Night stars paused in their twinkle. And it was as if the month, like Rachel, were holding its breath. Work went on. And, yet, there prevailed a sort of stillness . . . a waiting . . .

It seemed fitting that on Independence Day U.S. Marshal Hunt should bring the news that Oregon was nearing statehood. He had left on a combination business trip concerning political status which would affect the joint-ownership Cole insisted upon for the settlers and personal business. He would attend the legislature in Oregon City, thence to Portland.

"Seems th' Marshal's wantin' his wife t'join him— leastwise, that's the talk roundabout th' hotel," Aunt Em confided. "But Lucretia—that's her name—is a dyed in th' wool Bostonian. Appears he's got hisself another Mary Washington, accordin' to th' General."

The women looked at one another in understanding. Their men would come first, last, and always.

When the Marshal arrived, Lucretia was not with him. He spent 30 hours riding in from Oregon City, a dangerous journey, Cole said, looking at the sweat-lathered horse and shaking his head.

But the Marshal's usually expressionless face showed signs of excitement. The men gathered around him. Was it settled? When was the date? Oh, they were all interested!

Naturally. Except that their interest and their questions were in regard to mining. The Marshal's responses were in regard to statehood. Local quarrels had developed, he said . . . lots of trouble with the "Salem Gang" . . . not really safe. But a first vote cast for statehood looked promising (smiling) even though the circumstances were—well, a bit devious. Most of the opponents were playing in Wong's Tin-pin alley and "tilting a few" when the vote was called for. But a majority, mind you!

There was no great cheering. The men waited silently.

It was Brother Davey who walked up to stand beside the Marshal and, looking a bit like a bantam rooster addressing a giant Rhode Island red, stood on tiptoe and whispered something.

Oh, the papers? Why, yes, they were here in the saddlebag. Unofficial until signed and returned, but—

And the cheering came.

• • •

Usually on the first day of school Rachel felt a surge of excitement meeting the children who would belong to her, Yolanda, and Aunt Em to mold into the Christian citizens their parents so coveted for their learning. But this year she could think only how short—and how incredibly wonderful!—the summer had been. It was hard to believe it was over, she thought, as she welcomed them back—watching all the while as an occasional russet leaf fluttered down. A reminder that summer had come and gone. And all the while she was listening as well—listening to the sounds from Superstition Mountain where the first diggings were in progress.

For now—but not for long—Cole came home at night, although he was too spent to share much of the day's activities. Was all going well? she wondered. And even little Star, who curled into an egg-shape against his chest and counted his heartbeats aloud, grew silent after a while.

There were luminous nights when the autumn moon swung in the sky like an enormous, golden jack-o'-lantern—nights which she longed to beg him to walk through and share with her. Talk with her. But time for her seemed to have disappeared with the leaves of summer. Another of Aunt Em's "seasons of love," she thought. And with it came a greater understanding. The time would come, Cole promised, when they would be together forever here. Rachel clutched the thought to her heart where she kept the other thoughts tucked away. The thoughts—no, the realities which were more than thoughts—the reminders that even his divided attention could not be hers forever. And never, *never* would she change things even if she could. Not if it meant changing Cole's dreams.

Then came the night when Cole drew her to him and said softly, "I must ask you to make another sacrifice, Rachel."

"You're going away." Her voice was lifeless.

The billion stars she could see from the cabin window lost their light. Their energy, like hers, was spent.

But Cole was pulling the double-wedding-ring quilt tighter around them as if to reaffirm their vows. "I will never go away, Rachel—never, unless the Lord wills it—for any longer than I can help!" The words were wrenched from him.

"Then—what—?"

"Only some of the nights, now and then. We may,

just *may*, be nearing a strike. But let that be our secret!"

Rachel wound her arms around his neck, burying her head against the solidity of his chest. He would never know that her joy lay less in his news than in his promise that their separations would be brief.

The next night he was unable to get home. The night following he came home at midnight. But never once did Rachel complain. She treasured each moment, then wept when Cole—wonderful, caring Cole—began leaving quickly-scribbled love messages inside lopsided hearts on the dining table when he was up and gone before she awakened.

"My father loves us, yes?" Star's eyes were stars indeed.

"Your father loves us—*verdad*!" Rachel said, taking Star into her arms.

"Then we must pray for him, Mother Mine."

The two of them knelt beside the bed, their arms wound about one another, and prayed for the man God had given them to rule over their household—and their hearts.

• • •

Such busy times! Cole was away and perhaps did not see. Rachel, buried in her own thoughts, perhaps saw but attached no meaning to the sudden change in the settlement.

It was the children who commented on the activity. "What is it?" they asked of Rachel.

And then she realized that, although the men were gone, there was more noise—and, yes, less peace—than when they were here with their families.

Every day the road was thronged. There were immense freight wagons drawn by six to eight yoke of oxen, and towering Marietta wagons drawn by six span of horses. Bell teams! Then there were the long trains of 50...60...70...80 pack mules, all following the bell mare in single file.

Yolanda faced her with a certain fear in her eyes. What was happening? Where were they all going? But both girls knew. Word had leaked out. Peace and safety as they had known it were gone. Robbers were to be feared more than the Indians.

Rachel was separating a clump of daffodils when Aunt Em tapped on the door and entered late one evening. The blossoms had been beautiful—cups of gold—and, in their bid for immortality, had left behind a million bulblets. Aunt Em smiled, "I've come t'borrow a cup o'gold. There's been a strike!"

15

The Ageless Truth

There was a tentative glow to the October sun, signifying somehow the end of a golden age. End? It should be only the beginning. Gold was no longer a dream outsiders ignored.

I should be happy, Rachel thought as she listened to Cole outlining the plans for full-scale mining on Superstition Mountain. A week had passed and already the exodus of Oregon's Tomorrowland settlement had begun. Soon this quest for gold would take men from their families as feverishly they left the fields, mills, and shops—revealing once again the ageless truth of God's warning where the root of all evil lies.

But Cole was proud of the achievement, just as she was proud of *him.* Not happy, but proud. Men like him must be rare indeed—men who had inherited great wealth and preferred a life of service, without striving for power, to a life of self-indulgent amusement.

"But this will take you away nights!" Rachel burst out.

Cole did not answer.

"More?" She whispered from where she was snuggled against his chest. "More separations? How long?"

"Weeks—whatever it takes."

Cole waited for her to absorb it. No panic. Just a deep penetrating concern. An acceptance of the inevitable.

His grasp around her tightened. *Good girl!* it said. But Cole did not see the blood rush from Rachel's face, the tears gather in her eyes, or the soft mouth set in a firm, resolute line. He was reaching for his mackinaw.

Her mind was trying to accept what her heart could not bear. *I've spent my happiest days*, Rachel thought. *Cole and I have been together . . . dreaming and watching those dreams come true . . . the shade of the other child slipped away and we expected the Lord to entrust us with another. Now the peak moments of our life have passed. I was riding on the crest of the wave . . .*

She could only nod numbly as Cole, jabbing his arms into his woolen jacket, continued to speak. "Most of the doors will be padlocked (*like my heart*, she thought), with only those holding essential supplies remaining open. A telegrapher will be arriving. And Rachel," Cole turned to her, "there will be one room left open with an unmarked door."

Rachel felt an odd sort of premonition. They were all taking a momentous step. Things would never be the same. Tomorrowland was no more. No more building. Digging instead. Waiting widows. In a village with unmarked doors . . .

"What's it for, Cole—the room?"

"Meetings. Private ones. That's why no identifying door."

Secret, he might as well have said. Otherwise,

there was the Meeting House. Rachel understood without being told. To the passersby Tomorrowland would be another deserted village. Nobody would guess that in that bare, obscure, loft-like structure—its unmarked door purposely left swinging open—Cole would be arranging grubstakes for the villagers. Vacant, it would go unnoticed, giving no hint of Council meetings, the presence on occasion of the dignitaries (the Marshal, the General, and the barefooted wheat farmer). Here the local miners would bring their tobacco pouches of gold dust or a sizable nugget for an official staking—one that nobody could undo—all without a hint to the throngs of money-mad ruffians clogging the rutted roads that the gold they would kill for was being mined from the mountain they thought useless. But was it worth the price they would pay?

"Cole?" Rachel's voice was without emotion. "Must you do this? Already you have enough money."

"But the others do not. Don't you see, darling, that what I want is to be of service to others? The Lord has allowed me more than my share. I am in a position to help the others here with us. Then—" Cole paused and Rachel saw the dream enlarge in his eyes, "*if* there is more, we must see that it is distributed elsewhere. The Lord is not giving us this mineral He placed in the ground. He is only letting us find it."

"But your dream was to build."

"I am building. We are all building together." Cole's voice was soft but determined.

Yes, the Lord had blessed him. With more than money. Cole had a rare and instinctive sympathy. He was a born leader—willing to listen to the viewpoints of those whose ideas differed from his own and to understand. Just as he listened to hers. But in the end he was prepared with the facts and knew how to present them clearly and logically. That was the part of him Rachel admired but feared—the art of persuasion.

Rachel sighed soundlessly. "What about the hotel, Cole?" she asked, folding one of his socks over the other.

Without realizing it, she had resumed her role as second-in-command. The other women would expect her to know the plans. They would lean on her for support.

Cole pinched his upper lip, considering her question. "Yes," he said, breaking his concentration, "the hotel must remain open. There will be a great need for lodging. What would I do without you?"

Rachel had not considered her question to be a suggestion, but she let the matter pass. She would rather think on his need for her and hers for him. But there was time for neither. Cole was looking about the room, concern written on his face.

"Where is Star?"

"Watching Brother Davey make flannel cakes—she and Moreover. He teased her, saying they were made from a blanket."

Cole did not return her smile. "Good. I wanted to say that I don't like leaving you and Star alone."

"We're not alone," Rachel said, bravely trying to hold back the tears.

Again he gave no sign of hearing. "Keeping the hotel open will serve as a purpose for leaving Brother Davey. There are more risks than I like to think about."

"You underestimate us women."

"You're a wonder, Rachel!" Cole's smile transformed his face, making it younger, more light-hearted. One kiss and he was gone.

From the front window Rachel watched her husband walk briskly down the windswept street which was beginning to darken from a silvery mist that had blown in. There was something eerie about the scene in spite of Cole's easy stride, his fine carriage, the proud way he carried his head.

Cole wedged his way through a crowd of men and entered the hotel. When he returned, the City Council and General Wilkes were with him. The group entered through the unmarked door and Rachel could hear them talking in low tones. They would leave after dark, probably in pairs, avoiding suspicion should there be onlookers or (Rachel's heart skipped a beat) a spy among them.

The Marshal joined them at sundown. Rachel heard him through the thin walls speaking of his wife. He wanted her here so much, but . . .

The dark came down. Rachel tried to count as she heard them leaving. Which horse was Cole's? When it was quiet, she turned away. "Men could love and ride away," her mother had warned.

16

Life Goes On

The night the men left was the longest Rachel could remember. She let out the hem of Star's favorite school dress and brushed the burrs from Moreover's fur, grateful for the presence of the great wolfhound.

Star had trouble sleeping. "My father, he will be safe. Yes?" She asked over and over.

Rachel ruffled the child's hair with fingers that trembled slightly and tried to reassure her. But as she put dried beans to soak for tomorrow's dinner and darned Cole's socks, she heard the soft padding of Star's feet as she went to the front window to kneel and pray. *I should join her*, Rachel thought, but she did not feel like praying. So many of her prayers had gone unanswered.

So, instead of praying, she looked out the small kitchen window, eyes searching the dark trail that had taken Cole away again. If only she could see a star to wish upon. But the clouds had closed together as tight as brushed wool around Superstition Mountain.

Agnes could very well be right. Evil could lurk in and around the abandoned mine. Even Cole had indicated risks. And then ridden away. For a fleeting moment Rachel knew a cold fury that no amount of love and compassion could soften. Then she put ugly thoughts behind her. Situations like this were sure to tug at the weakest link in the nature of mankind. She must be able to greet the other women tomorrow with a serene countenance. The last thing they needed was a whining, worried wife of the leader. The lives of their husbands lay in his hands.

The brushed-wool sky turned a slow, thin pink. Dawn. And she had not been to bed. But a stirring below told her that most of the others had not either. Putting the nightmare hours of the night behind, she joined them. There was little indication of her stress except for the ashen look of her otherwise flawless complexion. A new way of life was beginning. She must make it as tolerable as possible. If only she could shake the feeling that tragedy lay ahead.

● ● ●

Brother Davey had his first chance to act in authority the first week. He was barring up the doors of the village and whitewashing them CLOSED when a barge tied up at the natural inlet serving as a harbor and a bedraggled crew, led by a bearded man in a sea captain's cap which had been white at one time, interrupted him. Rachel, who was standing near the door of the classroom, felt fearful at first. But they seemed friendly enough and her fear subsided, except for a feeling of uneasiness. She hoped Brother Davey would not forget himself and talk too much.

He didn't. The men were full of news, so, surprisingly, he listened instead of talking. "Lots of gold strikes on down the river a ways," the Captain said. "All in need o' supplies. Could use a few timbers, too. We've got th' cash money . . ."

Brother Davey kept nodding and soon the men were loading the barge and, after a hearty meal of Aunt Em's "sow belly 'n sourdough biscuits"—"and them was th' talkin'est men ever"—the crew embarked and drifted on down the river.

Brother Davey then made the rounds from door to door announcing a prayer meeting that evening. There would be others, he said, "often as th' Spirit moves us—'n when there's news."

Lots of steamboats would be transporting freight and passengers now. Sailboats, too. Then there would be "Portage Railways" (Brother Davey's eyes looked very wise as he shared).

"Portage Railways, Davey?" Aunt Em looked at him raptly.

"Businessmen puttin' 'steps' 'round th' navigable parts o' this mighty river. Railway trains drawed by mules. So th' river's no safer fer transportin' you-know-what. Makes one wonder 'bout Blue Bucket Mine . . ."

No more talk of the "Pacific Republic," Brother Davey went on to say. Statehood near at hand. Folks not much interested in the wars and rumors of wars. Closer at hand were Indians on the warpath . . . gold strikes . . . and how people were going to live with men running away from the farms the way they were.

All important matters, Rachel knew. But her mind kept going back to the report of the increase in navigation and the "Portage Railways." By "no safer" Brother Davey had meant that the waterways were no longer a protection if and when there was a sizable amount of gold to transport. Cole had been gone a week and the Oregon Country was changing already. The "first settlers" would have to alter their ways. The discovery of gold in California had caused excitement and change enough, but the discovery of gold close to home was still more fatal to the settlement. The old days were gone forever. The realization sent a shiver down Rachel's spine.

The hotel was kept busy by the flurry of travel, so busy that Aunt Em no longer had much time to help Rachel and Yolanda at school. Amity no longer seemed a fitting name, Rachel commented to Yolanda. "Neither does Tomorrowland carry much meaning for our town when we don't know if there's going to be one," her friend replied with a touch of sadness. And what was the other look? Regret?

"Be one what?" Rachel tried to make her voice light.

"A town. Or a tomorrow for that matter."

But the tomorrows came. Busy ones. The women were overburdened and they all sensed that the worst was yet to come. Rachel, however, was glad for the overload. It kept her mind off her loneliness for Cole and fear for his safety.

The women drew closer together as if there were safety in numbers. Hurrying ahead of the first frost, they made the last of the green tomatoes into sweet relish. They spaded up the Irish potatoes and the yams for the root cellar. And the late fall apples and ripening pumpkins they packed away in straw. Prunes were shaken from the trees and dried, and eggs were put down in crocks of water glass. Brother Davey ("struttin' 'round like a new rooster in th' hen house," Aunt Em observed affectionately), forgetting about his weak back and gout, cut and stacked winter wood alongside the Meeting House.

The scene appeared deceptively normal except for the haunted look in the white faces—and the gun Brother Davey carried wherever he went.

The telegraph office opened in the hotel. The telegrapher, a tight-lipped man, his face hidden behind a sunshade, was a disappointment to Brother Davey who openly declared himself "longin' for some man company" (to which his wife, nodding toward the other women, said, "Ain't they all?"). Not to be distracted, Brother Davey demanded all sorts of identification from the newcomer.

Actually, the telegrapher's quiet manner and seeming efficiency were a comfort to Rachel. Only she, too, wondered if Cole had had an opportunity to check his credentials, then scolded herself for being suspicious.

He would handle the mail, the man was saying. More regular delivery now with boats being more dependable than horseback riding. And was there anything else he could do for Mrs. Lord?

"You might tell me your name," Rachel smiled.

The weathered face beneath the sunshade remained immobile. "William Mead," he said.

William Mead. The name sounded innocent enough. But he would have access to all news and information between the settlement and the outside world. And he was a stranger.

November was a grim month. The rains had set in for the winter, muddying the roads and making it impossible to get the washing dry. The quilts would have to go until spring, the ladies agreed. The mail brought the first newspapers seen in some time. Rachel and Yolanda were the only two who paid much attention. Certainly, there was no great cheering. And neither of the two girls who had grabbed at the outdated papers ("before Ma papers the kitchen with them," Yolanda giggled) saw

William Mead motion with his head for Brother Davey to join him, where they talked in low tones.

Columbia had been cut away from the Territory and renamed Washington, Rachel read. Oregon was sure to be next. Probably by February. That meant electing a Governor, choosing a Congress, and no more money from the federal government. Rachel's mind flew to the added problems Cole would face in building. But Yolanda, leaning over her shoulder, asked a little too casually if there would be a change in the laws. And the telegrapher was telling Brother Davey that "these parts mustn't allow the news to travel so slowly as Washington had. Took a month. Traveled overland by that new stage to San Francisco, then up coast by ship to Portland. Young man saddled a horse there and took the news on. Might be the cover we need." Change in laws . . . cover in traveling?

Rachel wondered later how she could have missed the two cues. But at the moment they meant nothing.

The first telegram was a warning. More Indian outbreaks. The Salem Gang was not satisfied with the "government's meddling." The militia might be called in if robberies and killings over gold continued.

Rachel's spine prickled and Yolanda's eyes grew round with concern. But there were a few letters from "back home," and the other women had gathered to share the dream-filled messages. Mostly, friends and family wanted to join them here. And that night, as they quilted in the flickering lamplight that drove the dark into the corners of the Meeting House, they wondered what to tell them. Their questions were directed at Rachel, but she hardly heard the talk. In her heart she was marking off the days in her almanac. She needed to meditate and to pray. But God seemed far away—like Cole.

17

Warning Light

The busy days were bearable. The lonely nights were not.

Rachel's life had taken on a temporary routine and then it became fixed. In trying to juggle a dozen jobs at once, keep Star as happy as possible, and manage a somewhat false serenity for the women around her, some of the fear dwindled. But the loneliness remained.

She banked the fires of her heart as the days moved on. Marriage, as she had known it, seemed but a dream. Lying in bed at night after finishing her schoolwork, with Star sleeping, the thought was frightening—even bewildering. At those times she would twist the ring on her left hand. Touching the quaint Tiffany setting rekindled the embers of recollection. Cole would come home to her safely. Maybe even now...

And, barefoot, she would run to the kitchen window to peer into the dark shadow cast by Superstition Mountain. There was always a trembling hope that a familiar figure—walking at first, then running—would appear.

On one such night, Rachel thought she heard the faint tinkle of a bell. It came from the direction of the river. Quickly, she ran to the front window. It had snowed lightly during the night, leaving little stars of straying flakes against the windowpane. At first, she thought she only imagined the light. It was easy to lose one's sense of direction when the whole world was sifted in white.

Then in the quiet of the night the bell sounded again. Distinctly this time. And the light, swinging rhythmically, came into focus. In the middle of the river?

Rachel ran across the floor to the door, grabbed a jacket, and let herself out. There she paused to adjust her eyes to the darkness. The cold cut through her nightgown below the jacket and she realized that she had brought no weapon. At least she could have picked up the fire poker.

But when the light swung from right to left again, she raced toward the hotel, crashing headlong into a figure that loomed out of the dark. There was no time for fear. Dazed for a moment, she was suddenly steadied by two hands.

"Mrs. Lord!" There was surprise in William Mead's voice. "We must get inside—*quickly*. They're here—the men who warn seafaring vessels falsely of danger, then rob them!"

Then all the old fears came back. There *was* danger...

18

Cole Must Know!

The next day the sky cleared and briefly the arms of every bush and tree were packaged with snow. The long irregular rail fences twisted and coiled like giant, white snakes across the countryside. Rachel woke Star early to see the glory of it all. While the delighted child fell laughing to the ground to make a snow angel for the other children to find, Rachel searched the spot where she had seen the warning lights. They were gone, of course, but to her horror she spotted footprints—a man's, judging by their size—leading from the river. She held her breath, almost feeling their pause, as about halfway to the hotel they stopped and returned to the river.

"Mrs. Lord?"

Rachel jumped at the sound of Mr. Mead's voice behind her. Only the two of them knew about the lights, as far as she was aware. "I hope we can keep what we saw last night between us," she said quickly.

"Wise. Until time comes."

Rachel stiffened. "For what?"

The man lifted his sunshade and ran ink-stained fingers through his thinning hair. The round face was bland. His eyes gave away nothing, but Rachel knew instinctively that they saw everything.

He replaced the sunshade. "I'm speaking of the shipments—if and when."

Rachel caught her breath. "You knew?"

"Naturally." His voice was low and disciplined.

Yes, Cole would have chosen a man of this calibre —and she was certain now that he had done the choosing. Sending and receiving messages requiring such confidentiality was a lone-wolf job.

"You're saying the river's no longer safe?"

William Mead's eyes narrowed. How stupid of her after last night. "I agree," she murmured and motioned for Star.

The December sun suddenly blazed. By the time the school bell rang the snow had melted into small puddles. Star's angel and the footprints were gone.

Three days later word reached the settlement that a ship had been looted, the men beaten, and quite possibly several of the crew left to die as the crippled vessel floated toward the rapids that ran to the sea.

Rachel felt frozen. It was as if a jagged iceberg ringed her heart. Cole. . . . she must see Cole . . . gold must travel inland. Cole must know!

19

Dark Journey

"Davey 'n Willie, as Davey calls him, think it's best us women wear pants if it's absolutely essential we be outside at night—less'n we're in male company."

Aunt Em bent down to bite a thread from a quilt block, waiting for the gasps of horror to dwindle. Women in men's clothing? Why, it was against the teachings of the Good Book...totally out of the question. Why, it downright revealed the shape of the human body!

"I ain't doin' it. I got a mind o'my own...a body o'my own...a strong will..."

"And a big mouth!" Aunt Em said sharply to Agnes Grant. "Now, you be listen' t'me, Aggie, either you do as the men folks say, else you stay away from the quiltin' bees."

"You'll be telling us why?" Nola Lee asked quietly.

Yolanda stole a look of appreciation at her mother. The years of caring for 12 children had blessed her with serenity that comes from a deep faith.

" 'Twill make it look like more men's 'round here

in case snoopers 'n scalawags go gettin' th' idee we're helpless!"

When Rachel realized all eyes were turned questioningly to her, she nodded. Then, as voices indicated acceptance, she stole away on the pretext of making tea.

Yolanda followed. "You're going to Cole, aren't you? To warn him about the danger on the river."

Never able to keep a secret from Yolanda, Rachel nodded again. "If I can get you to keep two items— my daughter and my secret."

As they returned to the Meeting House in the darkness, each buried in her own thoughts, the night air was split by a scream. Agnes Grant! Rachel had not seen her come out, but it was obvious what brought the screech. The light Rachel and Willie Mead had seen a week ago was back. Back and forth it was swinging from some invisible raft.

"Rim o'fire! It's sent down from th' mountain to destroy us all. Breakin' th' law like you're proposin'. We'll be punished. Robbin' the dead . . . wearin' men's clothing . . ."

Rachel's heart sank as she saw Aunt Em rush to the hysterical woman. The reason for trying to make it appear that men were greater in number was no longer a secret.

● ● ●

Hannibal was surefooted, Rachel (dressed in a pair of Cole's work overalls, heavy jacket, and hair tucked beneath a discarded hat) remembered. If any animal could make it up the rugged trail, the stallion could. But she also remembered how steep and narrow the trail was. He had never made the perilous trip to Superstition Mountain at night. And the blackness was heavy and threatening. She tried to remember if horses could see at night.

Then concern turned to heart-stopping fear. Someone was following her. Not only following, but gaining. Rachel could hear the panting of another horse. It couldn't be her imagination, she knew, when Hannibal snorted and all but stopped on the narrow ledge.

"Not now, boy!" Rachel begged, unaware that she had spoken aloud as she urged Hannibal forward.

The hoofbeats were immediately behind her now. Desperately, she reached into her coat pocket and drew out the pistol General Wilkes had insisted she learn to fire.

Not that she would use it . . .

And then there was a low laugh. Yolanda!

"Some spy you'd make," Yolanda whispered, "talking aloud to your steed!"

Rachel's relief was so great she almost fell from the horse. "What are you doing here, scaring me half out of my wits? You were supposed to stay—"

"It was dangerous for you to come here alone. And Star's all right. She's with Ma. *Shhhh*—"

But the warning came too late. The outline of two men, barely visible against a low-burning campfire, loomed out of the darkness and, with what seemed to be one powerful move, the girls were swept from their horses. Of course there would be guards. Or was this the enemy?

20

Behind the Unmarked Door

Rachel dared not breathe. The night was too quiet. And she was too far gone. Mist, no longer parted by the movement of the horses, closed in around the captors and their captives.

It seemed hours. Actually only a moment passed. And then somehow Rachel knew. Yolanda's recognition must have come at the same time. And then the four of them, Rachel and Yolanda, Cole and Buck, had formed a tight square knot of relief, joy, and something closely akin to anger.

The girls were laughing and crying at the same time. And even in the pitch dark, Rachel could have vowed there were tears mingled with the men's voices as the four of them scolded, questioned, accused, and then soothed as they drew together again—hardly aware of whose arms held whom. They were together. They were safe.

Then Rachel felt Cole's lips on hers. Firm but brief. "You little adventuress! You *could* have been killed!"

Rachel might never have stopped crying had a sudden fury not crept in to rescue her from drowning.

Then she found herself saying the words, so long pent up, that she had not planned to say at all.

"You never contacted me. You didn't care how I felt. You could have been *dead*. Or *I* could have. Little you would have cared—"

Cole did not answer. He only held her closer until her tears stopped. Then he said softly, "I'm so sorry, darling, so sorry. But we were on our way home."

Home. Cole was coming home. Rachel tried to apologize, floundered, then tried again. But Cole did not seem to hear. He was helping her (and submissively she obeyed) astride the powerful stallion and mounting behind her. She leaned against him, trying to recapture, be it ever so briefly, the sense of sweet adventure of their wild night rides. But something else had taken its place. A certain sense of urgency she felt in her husband. Their time together during the past year had turned a courtship into a marriage. She had learned his moods and how to cope with them, knowing by the set of his mouth whether things were going well with the building— and later with the mining—plans. She knew whether to brew coffee so Cole could share. Or whether to keep silent, turn back the covers so he could rest, and stroke the fine lines between his eyes until he slept. Now was a time for quiet. Not because Cole did not want to talk, but because it was safer not to.

Over his shoulder Cole told Buck quietly it would be best if he and Yolanda rode Tombstone double so that one of the other men could ride his horse down. Ordinarily, Yolanda's sharing a horse with Buck would have been an item. As it was, Rachel's mind was busy with the news that some of the other men would be going down the mountain, too. Something big was in the offing. Just as it was in the settlement. But for now they were going home.

In the darkness Rachel felt Cole's chest expand with a deep breath. Audibly, he exhaled. He was relaxing and she knew that they had reached the floor of the valley.

"Almost home—*home*, how good that word sounds. Do we still have the wooden tub? I need a week's soaking."

Rachel laughed, forcing herself to relax. "It's hanging on the peg outside the back door and put to good use, I might add. Think your two girls would postpone baths until you got home?"

"*Home!*" Cole tasted the word again, his arms tightening around her. "Tell me, has anything been happening?"

Had anything been happening? "You never asked me why I came up that mountain all alone—until Yo followed—"

"Because you love me?" Cole asked innocently. Then, sobering, "Is Star all right—nothing's happened?"

"Star's fine—oh, Cole, wait until you *see* her schoolwork—we've a genius on our hands! But to say nothing's happened—oh, Cole, you have to know—"

She told him all about the strange lights, their meaning, and the hijacking of the ships. Cole listened in silence. It was hard to tell if he knew already. But one thing she knew. He *cared!* He was holding her so tight it was hard to breathe.

And suddenly they were home. Star and Moreover rushed out to meet them, neither paying attention to the callings of Nola Lee and Aunt Em. "Dad-dee . . ." and then the three of them were talking at once. Cole's bath could wait.

• • •

The next night Rachel sat alone in the livingroom. The drapes were drawn. The lamp was turned low.

Instructions from Cole were for her to use extreme caution while he attended a meeting. She knew the subject and it made her uneasy. Even the joy of being together last night had lost a little of its sheen when, after she had caught Cole up on happenings here, he had told her haltingly it appeared that there was even more gold in and around Blue Bucket Mine than at first thought. The awful ache returned.

Rachel snuggled closer, her forefinger tracing little hearts on Cole's chest while her own heart throbbed in her throat, causing her voice to tremble as she spoke.

"That means making sure claims are in order."

"And taking in proof."

"Gold? Inland—it's dangerous, Cole. You said so."

"We have no choice now," Cole had reminded her.

Rachel stopped in mid-outline of a heart. And, hardly aware of the movement of her forefinger, she traced an arrow straight through the middle, splitting the imaginary heart in half. But resolutely she said nothing. She would fight with Cole about it no more.

Not that her silence convinced him. Warily, he said, "Rachel, I'm sorry I have to attend the meeting then go away, but this is the biggest project we've ever had—important to the entire settlement." He paused.

But what about us, Cole? He would be the one to go, of course.

"I know," Rachel said tonelessly, conscious that each of them was walking on eggs for the other. *But I reserve my right to hate it!*

It was almost as if Cole heard. "Darling," he confessed, pulling her now rigid body to him, "I knew this could happen. But, believe me, I never foresaw the work involved, the separations. Rachel, I love you so much."

"I know," she said again... and now he was gone.

And the clock ticked on and on. Rachel, unable to read or grade papers, looked out the window time and time again. Nothing moved in the street. And the only light was that of the stars. Like distant chariots of fire in the night sky, they portended a bright tomorrow of foreverness. But this was Oregon country. The weather was unpredictable. Nothing certain but change.

Suddenly Rachel could no longer bear the waiting. "I am a part of this by no choosing of my own. The only woman who dares step out of character," she said aloud to the dog as she buttoned herself into a long woolen coat. "You watch over Star."

The great dog, wagging his tail, moved over to curl up beside the sleeping child. "Good boy," Rachel said as she secured the latch and stepped out into the darkness.

The unmarked door, usually open, was closed. Behind it there was silence. Rachel hesitated. It was absurd to have this strange reluctance. She had attended the otherwise all-male meetings before (shocking the women even more than it did the men). Nevertheless, she was relieved when Cole himself came to the door in response to the knock.

She was surprised to feel herself trembling. What on earth had she expected? A den of thieves... the robbers who swung lanterns at night... lions to be unleashed for devouring the Christians? *Get a grip on yourself*, she warned silently as Cole took her hand, led her to the nearest table, and made room for her to sit beside him.

A few of the men stood, General Wilkes among them. The others, deeply engrossed in conversation, did not look up. A quick look around the room told Rachel that she was among friends. The three men sitting at the far end of the bleak room were the General, the Marshal, and Burt Clemmons. Behind them, Yolanda's father, Judson Lee, the Honorable Lord Mayor...O'Grady...Farnall...Burnside...Sanders...and Buck, who was waving at her, a welcoming smile on his rugged face. The decision makers.

"What's said and done here's not to go beyond this room," one of the men in the back said warningly.

"Any questions before votin'?" That was Mr. Lee.

No need talking any more (although all were talking at once). 'Twas best choosing an "ordinary man," a man who was "one of them, loyal to God and country." One whose comings and goings would not be questioned...someone ordinary-like...

Rachel's heart sank. Her breath came in little short gasps. The discussion revolved around the taking of gold by the inland route all the way to Portland. And there could be no doubt as to their choice. She squeezed back the tears and waited.

Then, to her complete surprise, William Mead escorted in Brother Davey. *Brother Davey!* Could that possibly mean—? But before Rachel could finish the thought, Judson Lee, serving as moderator, boomed, "All in favor, so signify by sayin' 'Aye.' Opposed, 'No.' The 'Ayes' have it." General Wilkes was standing to make the announcement.

"Now, we cannot order you, Mr. Galloway. We can only request, feeling you're the right man. But you've a choice."

Brother Davey stood as tall as his stature allowed. "Me, I'd a choice when the Lord called me, too.

But He needed me. Me, I serve where I'm needed—"

Chairs scraped back. Rachel could not deny the surge of relief. And yet her heart went out to Aunt Em...

21

Arrivals and Departures

Rachel wanted to talk with Aunt Em, but there was no time. Uncle Davey left the following day, secret samples of the gold and proper instructions stitched inside his raincoat—the saddlebags (the first place robbers would look) filled with jerky, hardtack, and milled coffee.

A telegram advised that an assayer had headquarters in Champoeg, fast-growing townsite since the *Honolulu* entered the river, tied up, and bought up all the picks, pans, spades, knives, and flour. Could be mining folks could be accommodated here, unless the river was swollen by rain and couldn't be crossed. Well, the men would decide.

Men? Yes, the Marshal was going to Salem, probably the future capital city (if the Catholic and Protestant missions could behave themselves!). Word had it that the Marshal would be bringing Lucretia back with him—news as exciting to most of the women as David Galloway's mission was to the men. Business they left to their husbands. But now, a woman from the outside world, that was different.

114

Except to Rachel, Aunt Em, and Yolanda.

Rachel heard Brother Davey's horse leave in the wee hours of the night. The next morning she hurried to Aunt Em, getting to the hotel as she was laying the fire in the great kitchen range.

"I'll brew coffee," Aunt Em said as calmly as if it were any other day. "You know, all my Davey ever wanted was one chance, dearie. He got hisself that," she went on, face averted.

Rachel felt tears building up and overflowing. What a wonderful woman! Emmaline Galloway recognized a certain strain of frailty in her husband. And, knowing that there was a weakness in all mankind, she did not mind that her husband required her strong will to lean on. It did not alter her devotion. It strengthened it. It was she who had lent him the courage to take his coveted "one chance." Aunt Em poured two cups of her steaming brew.

"We'll pray 'im home—you, me, and his flock."

Rachel took a swallow of Aunt Em's strong, black coffee. It gave her the courage to nod. She wanted to tell her dear friend that she was no longer sure God heard her prayers.

• • •

Cole explained to Rachel that Timothy Norvall would be coming to the village to minister to the needs of the women. Rachel's only reaction was one of relief that there would be another male presence. Of course there was Mr. Lee, nearby as measured by the homesteaders but still too far as a means of protection in case of an emergency. But what was this? Judson would be going back with the men? After all, he had been one of the first to spot gold. His services would be invaluable. And now, darling Rachel would understand that Cole must be getting back. Sam Blevins and Ponce LaRue were alone at the mine. The engineer and surveyor had remained in view of the findings. Did Rachel understand?

Yes, darling Rachel understands. The parting was as unemotional as she could manage. After all, it was a solace that Cole was there instead of making the trip to Portland (or to that funny-sounding town).

Star and Moreover crowded between Cole and Rachel. Rachel was glad. It gave her a chance to avert her face. Cole needed no more tears. And this time when he was gone there were no tears either. Rachel was forming a shell about herself. Cole was gone. She was alone again. But Aunt Em and the others would need her. She must cope. Question: *Do YOU understand, Cole?*

There were surprising respites. Short visits—sometimes hours, one day when she and Cole escaped to a secluded spot by the river for a picnic, and two nights which were like a continuation of their honeymoon. But these hours of togetherness were too seldom and never long enough. All too quickly, Cole was riding back to Superstition Mountain, leaving Rachel to fight for survival...

• • •

Marshal Hunt returned to the village driving a carriage. He was immediately surrounded by children with great, round eyes. And not far behind stood their mothers.

"Probably the first such vehicle they've seen—women and children alike," Yolanda said to Rachel as she tried to shepherd the curious younger ones back into the classroom. "What's the occasion—? Rachel," she interrupted herself, *"look!"*

At first, all Rachel saw was Aunt Em who understandably sought news of her husband. Then her eyes came to rest on the stylishly dressed woman in black who sat beside the Marshal—aloof, unbending, and tapping her foot impatiently. Even beneath the plumes of the woman's oversized velveteen hat, an even mid-part showed in the blue-black hair (that Yolanda said later she would die for!). The rest of the raven hair rested in wings against a face so oval it seemed to have no bones. She wore a fur...

When Rachel realized she was staring, she quickly composed herself and hurried forward to meet the woman who was sure to be Mrs. Marshal. *Lucretia.* Yes, the name fit.

The gloved hand Lucretia extended when Rachel offered her own was limp. Rachel could almost feel the coldness through the long, suede glove.

"I'm afraid the rooms aren't exactly what a city guest might expect," Rachel smiled, forcing herself to be pleasant, "but—"

"There will be no problem," Lucretia said, each word a melting icicle, "I won't be staying."

Rachel helped Aunt Em take a feather bed and an extra quilt into one of the vacant rooms. Yolanda sent her oldest brother to the spring for fresh water to fill the water pitcher. Abe, shyly pleased to serve, ran all the way. Obviously accustomed to servants, Lucretia took no notice of the hospitality.

Oddly enough, the only woman Lucretia talked with was Agnes Grant. Undoubtedly, Agnes told as many wild tales as possible, adding the superstitions and half-truths in exchange for Lucretia's account of her trip—her own mind being somewhat imaginative, Aunt Em observed.

Aunt Em herself had gathered enough information to know that the inland trail was dangerous. The Marshal Hunts had been stalked. And Davey love may have been unable to cross at Champoeg. Water was high. Yes, he'd have maybe gone on to

Portland and "May th' Lord that made heaven 'n earth bless 'im if he did." But maybe he could file in Champoeg.

Lucretia refused dinner. She had a headache. She locked herself into the room prepared for her without bidding her husband goodnight. If he wanted to risk his neck going up that haunted mountain to report to equally foolish men, that was his business. The two of them would be leaving this forsaken place tomorrow.

That was to be the last any of them saw of Lucretia. On the way to "civilization," they were attacked by robbers. The Marshal, after filling out a complete report and seeing that a "Wanted" list of the faceless men (although one's voice was vaguely familiar— or maybe he imagined it) was posted, returned with the sad news. The taking of his wife's jewelry proved too much for her fragile constitution. Her memory was gone and her mind wandered. Doctors held little hope. White-faced, he requested prayer and went back to help the other men until he was called. Mr. Mead would notify him?

• • •

News of what happened to the Hunts increased the uneasiness among the "mining widows" as the women, starved for light words, named themselves. When a small mirror, hung low and near the window so Star could see to tie her hair ribbons, fell and broke, Rachel made the mistake of confiding to Aunt Em that the child's heart was as destroyed as the looking glass. Somehow the news reached Agnes Grant, who found an excuse to go from cabin to cabin to warn of seven years of bad luck. "It'll come—not jest to them high an' mighty Lords but to us all, livin' 'round 'em like we do. Th' Good Book warns us t'be avoidin' evil an' appearance of evil!"

So small an incident ordinarily would go unnoticed. But tension was high. Nerves were taut. Rachel could almost feel the women's fears mounting.

She felt a surge of joy and relief when the cheval mirror came. And, almost simultaneously, so did Buck! He had cut a bad gash in the palm of his left hand and Cole had ordered him down for a few days of rest. Aunt Em worried momentarily that the peach trees had lost their leaves. Then she substituted a mustard plaster for the peach-tree-leaf poultice. There were some light moments when Buck stormed about the hotel moaning, "If I thought the injury was bad, I should have known about the cure!"

His antics, partly to amuse Star, did exactly that—causing her to roll on the floor with laughter. When he "recovered from the treatment," Buck hung the mirror where the old one had been. One day the lovely mirror which once belonged to Cole's mother would be mounted on the washstand. The thought brought Rachel's dreams back briefly. Its very presence was a delight to Star. And its arrival put an end to the frightening prophesies of Mrs. Grant. "Somethin' sorta comfortin' 'bout that heirloom," Aunt Em declared. *And Buck's presence*, Rachel added in her mind.

And for the week he was there, she made the most of it. He seemed to sense the shell Rachel had formed about herself and to watch for signs of a crack. Knowing her as Buck did, he recognized that the world in which she lived was becoming too much. And so he spent most of his time in the Lord cabin.

Sometimes he played checkers with Star. Once he took Rachel, Star, and the dog fishing—blaming Moreover's sniffing out a rabbit too near the water for the fish's not biting. More often all of them, the day's work finished (Rachel and Star at school, Buck taking care of endless details around the village), would sit before the fire and talk. Carefully, they skirted mention of Cole's absence. It helped ease the ache of waiting. He could be in the next room...

Then came the night that Buck joined them for supper. "Red flannel hash—not much of a company meal," Rachel had smiled the invitation.

"I'm not company," Buck had smiled back and busied himself slicing a loaf of salt-rising bread.

This night was different somehow. There was a certain intimacy that was comforting. And yet it carried with it a sense of timing. *Be cautious*, Rachel's heart warned, *nothing is forever.*

She dished up the hash. Buck poured the coffee. And moments later Rachel recognized that her sense of coming change was not a figment of her imagination.

Star picked up her spoon then laid it down. "Do you wish to say grace, Uncle Buck?"

"Don't we always thank that Lord for what He has given us?" Buck asked her gently. But Rachel sensed that his eyes were on her instead of Star. The crack was in her faith.

"Well," the child hesitated, "sometimes we just *think* it, I guess. I mean, not always do we say the words—"

Buck reached for Star's hand and then Rachel's— squeezing hard as he prayed as if to share some of his strength. For a second, there was a flicker. Then it died.

Later Star fell asleep on the braided rug in front of the fireplace. Buck spread a small quilt over her, then set up the checkerboard.

"We've never played, you and I. Feel brave?"

Brave? No, I feel afraid. Abandoned...

But she left the words unsaid, seating herself across from Buck instead.

Rachel was winning when Buck said, "Better to quit when you're ahead!"

He wanted to talk to her. And she knew why.

"About what happened at the table—" Rachel began.

Buck, busy replacing the checkers in their box, did not look up. "It's what's happening in your heart that's important."

"I—I don't know what's happening, Buck. Those I love are so far away—even God. I can't talk to Him."

"Love knows no distance, Rachel darling. Remember that—even when I am gone."

"*You?*" The word was no more than a whisper.

Buck's laugh did not come off well. "Yes—I'm afraid I can't keep faking any longer." He lifted an unbandaged hand.

Rachel felt the knife of loneliness slice through her heart again. The wound had not healed when Buck rode back to Superstition Mountain two days later.

● ● ●

When an unfinished cabin near the Lee homestead burned mysteriously, Nola sent word of it by way of a note to her husband. Abe, who had become the village "runner" with messages, scrambled up the mountain, bringing his father back with him. He also brought an envelope which he handed, with some degree of importance, to Willie.

"Mr. Lord says it's t'be mailed at onct—" he panted. "I mean t'send a-uh—you know, telegraph."

There was little time for Rachel to puzzle over the incident. Judson demanded that his family "with less'n a kerchief o'worldly goods be movin' to th' village." Settling 13 people in was no easy matter.

Thirteen? Did they say *13*? Mrs. Grant prattled. Unlucky...unlucky.

"Her face's wearin' that sackcloth-'n-ashes look, but her tongue's happier than a dead pig in th' sunshine," Aunt Em said with a sigh to Rachel, then to Mrs. Grant, "Now, Aggie, don't go worryin'. Judson'll make 14."

"*If* he makes it again—if *any* of 'em do—"

"Here, give Nola a helpin' hand. Rinse th' Lee baby's diapers down by th' river before we boil 'em." Aunt Em handed the other woman a gunny sack of soiled clothing.

Agnes Grant hesitated. Then, meeting Aunt Em's commanding eye, she took the bundle gingerly and started toward the river.

"As fer th' men, they'll be home come Christmas —includin' my Davey love!" Aunt Em called after her. There was conviction in her voice, but none in Rachel's heart.

● ● ●

Aunt Em went about her duties with her usual calm bustle, mothering all. Rachel teased her about being the Old Woman Who Lived in a Shoe.

"Wonder if she had a man fer herself?" Aunt Em mused. And there was wistfulness in her voice.

It was then that Rachel began noticing how frequently in the midst of trimming a pie crust or telling a Bible story to the children that her friend raised her eyes to search the road that had taken Brother Davey away. Rachel wished she had asked Buck how long the round trip should take.

Yolanda should know. Her father made the trip to Portland once a year for supplies before the few trading posts and the beginnings of Tomorrowland met his needs. The two girls were working on a small Christmas program—Rachel, half-heartedly; Yolanda, for some strange reason, with more enthusiasm. A good time for an occasional word.

It was then that Rachel became aware that Yolanda, too, was watching the road. Strange, wasn't it, that she did not look the opposite direction toward the mountain trail which would bring her father and the other men home?

"Yolanda—"

Yolanda, who was looking at Star's manger scene and trying to help her decide whether the shepherds should be smiling, jumped at the sound of her name.

"Here!" She tried to say the word lightly, as if she were answering roll call.

"But your mind isn't."

"I was just wondering if he would be here in time for the program." Yolanda did not meet her eyes.

"Brother Davey? I was wondering, too—"

"I meant Tim—Brother Timothy. Don't tell me you didn't know."

It was Rachel's turn to feel confused. "I knew he was coming sometime. I guess I'd forgotten."

"Please, *Profesora*." There was pleading in the small voice.

"Oh, Star, I'm sorry. Let's give the men a smile."

In control of herself then, Yolanda turned back to Rachel. "He has been our guest several times." Yolanda let Rachel digest that before adding, "And he has reminded us several times at prayer meeting—"

Which you haven't been attending.

There was no accusation in Yolanda's voice. And already she had turned the subject back to Brother Davey.

"It never took Pa this long. Of course, there were a lot of details...but," she said slowly, "Brother

Davey should be back. Maybe it had something to do with the telegram."

The telegram! Rachel had forgotten the message Cole had sent for Willie Mead to put into Morse code. She had been too hurt that he had sent her no word at all . . .

When Timothy Norvall arrived, Rachel's first impression was that he looked a little less adolescent than she had thought.

He shook her hand cordially. "I hope I can be of some help here. I understand you are a born crusader—and Miss Lee—"

"Yolanda!" Rachel saw that Yolanda's cheeks were pink when she said her name softly.

"Yolanda here is a regular Florence Nightingale—"

"We'd better get at the Christmas music. The program's Friday." It was obvious that Yolanda sought escape.

Rachel was about to follow the pair into the Meeting House when Willie Mead waved to her and came hurrying across the muddy courtyard. "Response to Mr. Lord's telegram." He shook his head dazedly. "How could he just disappear?"

"Who?" The word caught in Rachel's throat.

"The preacher—that is, Brother Davey. In response to Mr. Lord's wire, there's no trace."

Brother Davey was missing? Rachel hardly heard Mr. Mead asking her to break the news to Mrs. Galloway while he fetched Abe. Mr. Lord would need to know. *And Aunt Em . . .*

Rachel's heart was heavy as she turned to the hotel. How was she going to tell Aunt Em? Surely if he were dead they would know. Oh no, no mention of that possibility . . .

"You'll have to help me, Lord," she whispered, surprised that she still knew how to pray. But when *others* were in trouble, maybe there was a difference...

• • •

U.S. Marshal Hunt accompanied Abe to the settlement. He, not Cole, would be making the trip to Portland. He must check on Lucretia in Salem... spend Christmas with her. Christmas was for families. Rachel nodded with a singing heart. But even with the relief and joy she felt, there was a corner of her heart that refused to release its fear. The real reason for Marshal Hunt's going, she knew, was that he was better skilled at procuring information. She was sure he suspected foul play.

She had no more than waved him goodbye, with tears flowing unashamedly down her face and a promise to pray for his safety and success, than Abe came to stand beside her, hands digging deeply into his overall pockets. His eyes were on the worn toes of his cowhide boots and his freckles stood out darkly in his pale face.

"What is it, Abe? It can't be that bad."

The boy's Adam's apple worked up and down, but he was unable to find a voice. Wordlessly, he handed her a crumpled note while fishing in the other pocket for something else.

With shaking fingers Rachel smoothed out the faded piece of paper, pressing it against the folds of her long skirt. One by one she made out the words.

I love my Bunny Face! Living for the day
we can be together. Your Cole.

"I'm sorry I forgot 'bout the note, Miz Rachel." Abe was still digging in his pockets, his embarrassment growing. "I didn't forget this time—honest!"

"It's all right, Abe." She assured the red-faced lad.

And it was. *Everything* was all right. Her heart had set Cole's note to music. The dark of the daytime sky was filled with stars. The raindrops were jewels standing on the stems of Abe Lee's red cowlick . . .

"Oh, here it is!" The boy was handing her a small metal object, cold but familiar, and Rachel was touching the freckled hand in appreciation. The cross, Cole's father's talisman when he went out to sea—now engraved with her initials beneath Cole's. Only she could not make out the letters. Her eyes were blinded with tears.

Strains of the Christmas carols sifted through the cracks in the log walls of the Meeting House. Rachel was glad Buck had forgotten to chink them up. The music was that of an angel choir, sent down to join in her joy.

"You'll send him home. You'll send Cole home for Christmas. I know You will, Lord—"

Rachel had not realized she was singing her prayer aloud until Aunt Em's arm was around her. She was wiping her eyes with her apron. There was a smudge on her nose. But her eyes were twin stars. "Th' Lord be praised, dearie, that *you've* come home!" She blew her nose on the corner of the enormous apron. "Of course, He'll send your Cole— 'n most likely my Davey! It's been a season of goin' 'n comin'—"

22

The Gift of Christmas

Rachel awoke early with a feeling of excitement. Oh, yes, the Christmas program tonight. But, no, it was something more. The children had asked for a hands-off production. Would the grown-ups please be a part of the audience? They had taken over on the decorating as well, wanting help on nothing except the music. And, yes, Brother Timothy should pray. All was done. And it wasn't the baking that gave rise to the feeling of anticipation. Sure that their men would be unable to leave the mine, the women had baked well in advance. Abe and two friends of his choosing would take the food as soon as the stuffed hens, put in the oven before dawn, were ready.

What then? Rachel passed the cheval mirror on her way to put the coffee to boiling. She looked at her reflection. Why, she was blushing—or was it a trick of the light? Practically, she picked up her hairbrush and began the 100 strokes on her silken hair . . .

It was unreal. And yet it was the most natural

thing on earth that Cole should be standing behind her, a head taller, his hands on her shoulders. So still they stood that the reflection in the great oval mirror might have been a photograph taken from some ancient album.

I knew...I knew...I knew, Rachel's heart was singing. Christmas was for families. This was preordained.

Cole took the brush from her hand. Wordlessly, as if it were happening to somebody else, Rachel watched the pantomime in the glass. The man's lips were moving.

"You should keep your door locked." His handsome face bent toward her. His eyes were amused, love-filled.

"I do—but I knew." Her words came out in a whisper. Her lips parted, waiting. His were close, so close.

Then his lips were on hers. Warm. Gentle. The way she remembered, would always remember no matter how long circumstances kept them apart.

The kiss was too soon gone. Cole turned her toward him, reading her face. "Merry Christmas, my darling!"

For one blessed moment he crushed her to him, burying his face against her hair. "You smell of pine needles—and apple blossoms—" Cole's husky voice became inaudible.

"We're decorating—pine boughs—" Rachel was gasping for breath, laughing while wanting to cry. "But apple blossoms—they're a season away. You're holding me so close—"

"I always hold you like this in my heart. Apple trees can bloom in any season for a love like ours."

• • •

Christmas Eve. Cole at her side. And their daughter playing out the old, but always new, story of the holy birth as the mother of the Christ child.

Rachel, in a dove-gray flannel dress with a ruffled pink collar which matched her pink cheeks, sat transfixed. Never had the blessed story been so beautiful. And never, Cole's eyes said, had *she* looked more beautiful. So obviously in tune with God. Buck need not worry...

"You look so pure, so demure, so untouched by the world," he whispered during a change of scenery. "A Madonna."

Rachel's blush deepened. And then she reached for his hand. It was as if her movements or her words were not her own. "If our next child is a girl, I would like to name her Mary—"

Cole's hand gripped hers so hard that she almost cried out in the wonderful agony of the moment... the moment she wanted to preserve forever.

Then the children were taking their bows to a cheering audience and Timothy Norvall was moving forward with an open Bible in his hand. He read St. Luke's version of the Christmas story.

"But the real miracle of Christmas is not only Christ's gift to us. It is our gifts to Him, ourselves. Our love for Him. And our love for one another."

Yolanda, in an old green wool dress (made new by a white lace collar with a sprig of holly at the neck), smiled at the young minister before her fingers struck up the chords of what must have been the fortieth carol.

The congregation joined in singing as Rachel and Cole, by prearrangement, slipped away. It was Aunt Em's idea that they have this moment together. The children would be removing and devouring the doughnuts, popcorn balls, and gingerbread boys from the tree. The parents having coffee...

This morning they had talked nonstop. Rachel was glad Buck had filled Cole in on the strange events

of the village. She added only a finishing touch of
words here and there, then listened to Cole with an
inner ear that read the spaces between. Some of the
other men would be down. They would have to take
shifts guarding the mine. She understood? Yes.
Cole's stay would be short then? Cole seemed eva-
sive, so she switched the subject to lighter matters
. . . the arrival of the mirror . . . Star's achievements.
Did Cole know she had drawn all the pictures for
the background? They talked of everything except
what lay heavy on their hearts: What had happened
to Brother Davey?

Now, they walked to the accompaniment of the
carols growing fainter and fainter in the background. There were no words. The moments were
too sacred to be violated by sound. Rachel was
remembering the contours of her husband's face,
the intensity of his eyes, even the heavy rhythm of
his chest as he breathed in and out in the candle-
lighted room, as they walked hand-in-hand beneath
the Christmas moon—the gift God had placed there,
the shining circle to symbolize the eternity of love.

23

Farewell with a Promise

In the morning Star was awake well before dawn. "*Feliz Navidad!* Merry Christmas! And please to open my gifts!"

The child showed no signs of fatigue, even though the three of them had stayed up until the great school bell was announcing with the clatter of its iron tongue that it was Christmas Day. Rachel did not feel tired either. Her world was still light and iridescent with the memory of last night's glory. Even as Cole responded to Star's wake-up call, Rachel stretched luxuriously, still wearing last night's smile.

A beautiful day stretched ahead. Dinner at the hotel with its special Christmas breads...the plum pudding blazing with the blue light that only Judson Lee knew how to make glow...the early-morning worship service which Rachel in her newfound relationship with the Giver of all good things welcomed with all her being...the *whole* of Love's season as expressed by God through the giving of His Son.

True, one dinner could not bring them all together

as it had in the past. But as the men came and went, there would be a day of constant greeting. Except for Aunt Em—

Watching Star tear the wrappings from a rag doll, stitched and stuffed by Aunt Em, and hearing her cries of delight as she cradled the treasure to her, rocking back and forth with joy, Rachel felt a pang of sadness. "Please, Lord, *please* let us hear something today," she whispered as she reached for her robe.

Rachel's prayer was answered almost immediately. Cole had poured the coffee and Star, wearing the red mittens Rachel had crocheted for her, was trying unsuccessfully to butter buckwheat cakes. Moreover, drooling, watching patiently for a generous section of a pancake, now swimming in syrup, to drop from Star's plate. A cozy domestic scene. One which could go on forever after, a mixture of buckwheat cakes and shining moons except—

There was a rap at the door. Somehow even then Rachel knew that her daydream was shattered. Cole's voice was all wrong when he greeted Willie Mead. And Willie's was too hushed on a bright Christmas morning when he spoke.

"The mail was held up, so Old Bill, who used to deliver by horseback, brought it on. Otherwise, no holiday mail—and you know how lonesome Christmas can be for the newcomers."

It was uncharacteristic of Willie to use more words than bare facts demanded. Cole, his knuckles standing out white against the latchstring in his hand, interrupted the flow. "Another piracy?"

Willie nodded. "Mail sack ripped apart and mail scattered."

Then, without further conversation, he placed two letters in Cole's hand. "Oh, and these for you, Mrs. Lord, Ma'm. And where's the Missy?"

Some faraway part of Rachel realized that Star had raced to Mr. Mead, taken the packages, and was embracing her father. That was good, Rachel thought vaguely. She herself could never have forced her limp hands to hold the mail-order packages, small though they were.

Without sitting down, Cole slit the envelopes while the faraway part of Rachel watched. "*Mi casa es su casa,*" Star said, opening the door wider in invitation to Willie. Of course. It was Christmas. It was Christmas, a time to make room in the inn. But Rachel stood frozen, her eyes on her husband's white face. *My house is your house. Words left unsaid.*

Ages later, Cole turned to Rachel. Pocketing the letters, "Aren't you ladies going to open your presents?" he asked.

Rachel fumbled with the wrappings and went through the empty ritual of taking the lid from a small box. Maybe she exclaimed. Who was to say? The center of her world lay in those envelopes, not here. A gold chain caught a shaft of the rising sun. Gold filigree. Gold—the root of all evil.

"It's for the cross—"

"I know." Rachel's words were choked with tears.

Star, holding her first box of oil paints to her heart, stopped in mid-pirouette. "Mother Mine always cries when she's happy," she said solemnly.

"So do I!" Cole said, taking a large handkerchief from his pocket and faking a loud blow. Star laughed with childish delight and went on with her dance.

"Tell me, Cole." Rachel's voice was a whisper.

"It's nothing, darling—nothing definite. It will be all right—"

"Just *tell* me."

"I must go to Portland," Cole began, reaching to take her in his arms. Rachel pulled away. "Go on."

The ringing of the bell summoning worshipers was a death knell. The carolers were mouthing a dirge. Star ran out to join her friends. And inside the cabin, Rachel listened—Cole's words running together foolishly.

Imperative Cole come, Marshal Hunt's letter said...must help settle the dispute of ownership surrounding Superstition Mountain...else all was lost. Cole *must* come. The other letter? Cole must help rescue Brother Davey (no explanation). His life at stake.

Even as they stood in the center of the room, strangers as it were, there was a rap at the door and through the window Rachel saw the sunlight reflecting on Willie Mead's sunshade. "Sorry to bother you again, sir, but there's a telegram."

A telegram. A telegram which said, "Urgent you come immediately."

No, Rachel could not go. It was too dangerous. He would return very soon to resume their dreams.

Something inside Rachel snapped then. Blood resumed its flow through her veins, letting her move. She sprang forward like a primitive animal protecting its own.

"Oh, Cole, no! I can't let you go again. I can't!"

Even as she fought to control the hysteria which had been building for two years, Rachel felt her hands clutching his shoulders as if, words having failed, her physical strength could hold him back.

"Rachel darling," Cole said, gently removing her hands, uncurling her palms, and planting a kiss in each, "try to understand—"

But Rachel was past understanding. "I wish we'd never come West—that we'd stayed where we had roots—where there was civilization—"

"My darling, no!" Cole held her tenderly, but his eyes, behind their sorrow of another parting, were bright with the light of adventure she had come to know so well. "We're in a new land and we must bring civilization to it. We must not allow the flaws of the flesh to deter us from the work God sent us here to do. Here we are measured by what we do, not be what our ancestors did. I'll be back—"

Be back? When? Once she had heard—actually *heard*—the voice of the Lord. She had not heard the words exactly—just the voice. Was He telling her she would be given no more than she could bear?

Somehow Rachel sat through the Christmas service, although she could not have told another what transpired. Somehow she helped serve the dinner, even managing a meaningless smile. And somehow she, washed, mended, and packed a change of clothes for Cole's journey while he met with the other men to explain his mission.

Tears were all right. She need not hold back when Cole mounted the black stallion. Hadn't Star said she only cried when she was happy? But the hurt was too deep for tears.

Only one thing got her through the goodbye. Cole's promise. "This," he said, "will be the last time I leave you." The words, so lovingly spoken, told her how much the parting hurt. And then he was gone again.

She looked around the room, already so lonely without him, and there on the table lay her gift to Cole. How could she have forgotten to give him the daily love letters she had written and Star had illustrated, then together they had bound into a book? Well, he would be back soon...

24

Survival

The year was brand-new. Two weeks passed, then three. Rachel plunged into it with a new determination not to mourn, repine, or allow dark thoughts to eclipse the glories of the world to come. Her world with Cole as its center. Neither must she fail in her duties here. Somehow she had managed to stem the bitter flood of grief inside. Or perhaps her heart had gone through a vise, squeezing it dry of tears.

Once alone, when Cole left, she thought she could sob and sob. But, strangely, not a tear remained. The icy ring congealed around her heart again as she set about picking up the wrappings from the Christmas packages. She was still tidying the room when there was a knock at the door. *Go away!* Her heart cried out and she locked herself in the kitchen where she could not hear the knocking or the sound of a voice.

And there she prayed until her vocabulary was as empty of words as her heart was of tears. But when she rose to her feet, she felt strengthened.

Going back into the living room, Rachel caught sight of a human form hunched on the doorstep. It was near twilight and she was uncertain whether it was a man or a woman, since the women continued to wear pants when dark approached.

Cautiously, she opened the door a crack and the form took shape.

"Buck! You've been here all this time?" Ashamed she opened the door wider.

Buck rose stiffly, a half-smile on his face. "I would wait forever. You know that."

"You knew?" She whispered, trying not to cry.

Buck nodded. "Cole sent Abe. Oh, Rachel, I'd have gone in his place if I could have."

The ring of ice melted. And then she wept.

● ● ●

How long would it be until she could expect to hear from Cole? The first thing she must do was see Aunt Em. They could comfort one another. Then she would brush and air Cole's best suit as if he would be wearing it Sunday. Get herself on a rigid schedule...

Aunt Em was churning when Rachel entered the hotel. Tossing the churn dasher aside, Aunt Em gathered Rachel in her arms. "Oh, little dearie, I know—I know. But here it ain't *me*, it's *we*. We'll make it—together, with God's help!"

And thus they had survived so far, dependent one on the other...

25

The Letter

"This is only temporary," Rachel said hopefully of the dark day.

The words had become the article of Rachel's faith. Everything was temporary. Even the mirror she looked into as she swirled her hair up into a temporary knot. Time allowing, she would do a better job before tonight when the people of the village gathered to say farewell to General Wilkes.

Rachel frowned at her reflection, half expecting her face to fade in the temporariness of other things. How pale she was! Pinching a bit of color into her cheeks, she turned to glance about the room.

One day everything would change. There would be permanency. She and Cole would have the big house built and filled with the new furniture, now wrapped in worn sheets, secured by cobwebs, and stored in the unoccupied rooms of the village. The cheval mirror would be mounted on the washstand . . . Mother's china cabinet dominating the parlor . . . the brass bed . . . and the roses (carefully planted to entwine the gateposts), now pouting with winter, would bloom in celebration of Cole's coming home as he had promised.

Until then, she must live in the mecca of the temporary. Even her pregnancy was temporary...

Yes, she was expecting a child. Buck thought her lethargy and fatigue were due to overworking. For certainly she was doing that. Aunt Em suspected the truth. But only Rachel knew for sure. It was her job to hold the village together until all the men were home and the valley once again bloomed and the ring of hammers and saws echoed sweetly against the canyon walls. She must hold herself together as well.

How would she have borne the loneliness without Buck? For this time she was less ecstatic over the thought of giving birth. Remembering her loss, her heart was filled with fear. And Cole was not here to reassure her.

But there was Buck. And there was Star. And there was the Lord! In fact, one would have a hard time separating the three of them. So often were they together. And so often were they in prayer.

Aunt Em, who was her usual self—her deep concern revealed only in the increasing telltale streaks of gray hair—remarked to Rachel how fortunate it was that Buck had taken over in Cole's absence. And not only with the needs of the villagers.

"I praise the Lord for him—a surrogate father to Star," Rachel said fondly.

"And surrogate husband, if ye ask me!" Agnes Grant, ever the eavesdropper, muttered.

• • •

Now there was a rumble of thunder, followed by a few drops of rain, and then a downpour. The drenching rain transformed the once-friendly trees bordering the bend of the village into strangers— giving the woods a gloomy, inhospitable look. Rachel was relieved when she saw Buck silhouetted against the bar of light in the hotel kitchen. He hesitated a moment then came striding toward her cabin.

Moments later they were sharing coffee, both of them unusually quiet. Buck laid down his spoon.

"What's troubling you, Rachel?"

"Buck," she said slowly, "what do you think has happened?"

"To Brother Davey and Cole?"

Rachel nodded mutely, then picked up the conversation. "Even the Marshal—his leaving and now the General's going. Is—is there a connection? Is there something I don't know?"

"There is a lot none of us know." That was one of the things she loved about Buck. He never patronized her. "But, yes—although he would deny it—I think there is a connection."

They finished their coffee in silence.

When Rachel let Buck out the front door she stood for a moment studying the landscape. The whole world seemed to be listening. The villagers listened for the sound of hoofbeats and the earth listened for spring.

February.

The month when winter should be withdrawing. But there was a reluctance—a reluctance to let winter go, and a reluctance to allow the arrival of spring. Surely this was the least lovely time of the year. The snow had gone (unless there was an out-of-season storm). There was Oregon's eternal green, but the buds had not yet appeared. There was a sort of desolation, and yet a mysterious stirring in the air and just below Rachel's heart. *Something tremendous is about to happen*, the silence seemed to say. But for the life of her, Rachel was unable to tell if it would be good or bad.

She must bake a cake for tonight. But, unable to concentrate on domestic things, Rachel found herself making repeated trips to the corner of the hotel designated as the post office.

"Not likely to be any mail today," Willie said each time. "River's high and apt to be another storm."

But just as she set the chocolate cake into the oven, Buck himself came to the door. Handing her an envelope, "I'll leave you alone with it," he said, "unless you want me to stick around—"

Rachel grabbed for the envelope and ripped it open with such eagerness that one corner of the letter was ripped off. Buck picked it up, handed it to her, and walked away without her seeing the concern in his eyes.

Cole! She had a letter from Cole!

The letter was warm, love-filled, but guarded. At first, her heart throbbed with the same old girlish thrill of the sweet phrases. Then the woman in her took over. Rachel read and reread the words. Looking for a clue as to Cole's whereabouts, his findings, his plans. But there was nothing.

Something was wrong. It was nothing he said. It was what he did not say. As Rachel read the letter for what must have been the hundredth time, she had a sudden strange sensation that the clue lay in the passage of Scripture Cole quoted at the bottom of the letter.

> The earth is the Lord's and all the fulness
> thereof,
> The world and those who dwell therein;
> for he has founded it upon the seas,
> and established it upon the rivers.

Who shall ascend the hill of the Lord?
    And who shall stand in his holy place?
He who has clean hands and a pure heart,
    who does not lift up his soul to what is
false, and does not swear deceitfully.
                                    —Psalm 24:1-4

The bell at the Meeting House rang. Rachel called Star. As she retied her sash and smoothed the dark bangs, "We had a letter from Daddy," she said.

The child's great, dark eyes were solemn. "He loves us, but he cannot come home. Yes?"

Rachel could only nod. And at the farewell party she could only force a smile here, a word there. But the others were doing the same. Their faces were grim. They knew...

Back home, Rachel read the letter again, and then again, as she was to do for a long time afterwards. For it was the last letter she received from her husband.

26

Three Come Home

March came in like a lamb. Gardening time. There had to be gardens, elsewise they would all starve, wouldn't they, Mrs. Lord. *Yes, yes, they must go on.* But how—with the men gone and all?

The waiting. Their men were only on the mountaintop while her husband and Aunt Em's were— yes, *where?* And yet she read an intensity about them. A need to share the pain. A need to know, to get on with their lives. They, too, were tired of waiting. Gardens were a security of sorts.

Buck, sensing the unrest, suggested that the miners come home. Oh, it was only temporary, he said. Just until the other men returned. Why not close the Blue Bucket Mine, store the gold . . .? Again he said it was temporary. With the mine closed, Ponce and Sam went their separate ways temporarily. There was no need for surveyors and engineers until the claims were legalized.

There was more concern than mumbling. The air filled up with the smell of newly plowed earth. And

142

the trellises hung heavy with clusters of wisteria, like purple waterfalls.

Superstition Mountain leaned against the cloudless sky. Silent. Lifeless. Except that the ravens had come back.

Rachel was looking up at the peak when suddenly it swam before her eyes then righted itself, still and unnatural as if painted there. She recognized the feeling. She had been working too hard, not putting the welfare of the unborn baby first. As she steadied herself against a tree, she realized she was not alone.

"See 'em? Spells trouble—as if you don't be havin' enough!" Agnes Grant . . . and her see-all eyes were sweeping over Rachel's body knowingly.

Rachel realized then that she must make an announcement. Already she could see Mrs. Grant counting off the months on her meddlesome fingers.

"I wouldn't be spendin' much time lookin' up yonder, what with them demons from Hades. Could be bad fer you. They've not come to th' abandoned mine fer nothin'!"

"The mine is not abandoned, Mrs. Grant." Rachel felt the blood hot in her temples but determined to remain calm. "It is only closed temporarily."

Temporarily. That word again. But the sentence was never finished. There was the sound of horses' hooves, men's voices shouting from afar, then bedlam in the village.

Cole! Rachel ran, stumbled, then ran again. Buck's hand steadied her. "Careful, Rachel. It's Hunt and General Wilkes. They've brought Brother Davey home. Maybe there'll be news—"

Above the buzzing in her head, Rachel heard Aunt Em scolding, "Get in here, Davey love. I've seen fatter scarecrows!"

27

Who Is the Enemy?

General Wilkes took Buck aside for no more than a minute. Then an emergency meeting was called. To Rachel it seemed that nobody—man, woman, or child—was missing from the village. Except for Brother Davey and Aunt Em. At first Brother Davey—exhausted, tired, and dirty—protested when Aunt Em insisted that he needed sassafras tea and "beddin' down." Him leave? Never!

He was the hero. The only one "what knowed" the story. "Why, them there foreigners 'cused me of bein' everything—one of them 'Oregon Men' er 'Columbia River Men'—"

"Names applied by the Mexican and South Americans to us Americans who seek gold," the General interjected.

"Some thought I was th' *law*—some thought I was runnin' *from* it . . . Indian lovers—them redskins is mad—and Indian haters—them whites makin' treaties is madder still . . . then there was th' hoodlums who was gonna hang me—*me*, a Bible-poundin' preacher. Would've, too, iffen I had'n told 'em I had a stiff neck...then showed 'em a bag o'gold..."

There was a moment's horrified silence in the Meeting House. Then Aunt Em managed to drag her husband away.

General Wilkes with his usual calm said that it would be wise if he and Marshal Hunt reconstructed the story, as best they could. They would combine what Brother Davey had been able to tell them with their own findings. Then, together, they would all assess the situation...find out, if possible, who was the real enemy.

When there was a low rumble of voices, Buck spoke up quietly but with a note of authority. "Let's wait until we've heard the story before making judgment. You have the floor, General."

The General cleared his throat. "First," he said quickly, "let it be known that Brother Davey, as he is affectionately known among you, *is* a hero of sorts. Second, the Marshal and I want you to know that finding him was no easy matter. He was hospitalized in Salem—head injury causing a temporary loss of memory. So there will be gaps in our account. Meantime, we beg your indulgence."

It was a time of unease, he explained. The Oregon people were unused to statehood, and self-government took a while to put into practice. There were to be new laws and decisions. Some of them an improvement. Some of them a curse. But all were controversial. Take the one concerning release of former prisoners—jails being overcrowded—

Rachel saw Yolanda's face blanch. It was then that she recalled Yolanda's interest in the changing of the laws when Oregon became a state. Somewhere out there in the still-untamed wilderness called Oregon, Cole was searching for Brother Davey, not knowing that he was safe. And Julius, the half-beaten enemy, roamed free.

No mention yet of Cole's whereabouts. And there was no need. If there were news, it would have taken priority. And yet Rachel found herself glancing periodically down the road, hoping against the impossible to see the great black stallion being reined in. Cole's hands reaching out to her. To lift her up beside him. And together they would once again ride away from all of this. Carefree.

But did she really expect to see him? No. Her expectations were more realistic now. The stress of day-to-day living—giving more to others than she kept for herself—could but wreak havoc with dreams. *But*, another part of her cried defensively, *dreams are not the heart of love. It is the people who weave those dreams . . . and work together making them come true against impossible odds, even in the dry seasons . . .*

Rachel came out of her reverie with a start. The General had mentioned her name.

"—having a wife with such simplicity and charm is such a definite asset to the man with a dream. And, then, what could be more valuable than such a loyal friend and colleague as City Manager Jones?"

There was a spattering of applause then a call for questions. Rachel listened intently, aware that she had missed some of the pieced-together information.

When would the mine be reopened? What could they do in the meantime? When would they know the truth—the *real* truth—surrounding the disappearance of their leader?

"The Council must decide much of this," the General said soberly. "I have had little time to confer with Mr. Jones—Buck—but I would suppose you will wish to continue life as normally as possible. Building, yes—planting and harvesting . . . leaving off with mining until there could be no question about ownership—"

He stopped and fingered his watch chain, fanning the fob from right to left, as if wondering whether to continue. Marshal Hunt took opportunity of the pause.

"Yes, I am in agreement. Tomorrowland—or have you found a new name?" At the general shaking of heads, he went on, "Tomorrowland should—*must*, in fact—look like any of the towns that are springing up, not a tent city and not exactly a Salem, Portland, or Champoeg, but growing with no purpose other than serving the needs of the wagon trains. Yes, after a period of quiet, more are coming, drawn by the cry of 'Gold in California!' And there'll be hordes of prospectors and miners which we want to sell to then shoo on to the south . . . *mum* being the word. Nobody must suspect that the 'Lost Mine' and 'Blue Bucket Mine' are one and the same."

There was a flurry of questions. Rachel strained to hear the answers. "Lost Mine was the name Brother Davey came up with when he was ambushed—"

Ambushed?

Correct. Ambushed and taken captive. But only after his caper at the Lucky Lady bar.

Bar? Brother Davey?

It was the Marshal's turn to hesitate. The General cleared his throat and nodded. "We told them Mr. Galloway—Brother Davey—was a self-styled hero," he said.

The crowd strained forward as Marshal Hunt gave the unbelievable account. "Brother Davey," he began, "is not the typical patron, it was easy for the regulars to see when he entered the Lucky Lady. He was in need of food, having been scared away from where he'd pitched camp by a group identifying themselves as 'Oregon Riflemen.' In his haste, he left his grub sack."

More was to follow. And the story grew more bloodcurdling.

One man in particular "kept eyein' " him, Brother Davey had said. He was sort of suspicious-like—even a little familiar, 'ceptin' that Brother Davey didn't have no acquaintance with a foul-scented man with a beard the birds undoubtedly nested in. May've fought with the British in the Revolutionary War. Coat bein' red, couldn've been a Russian diehard. At best, hard tellin' a Whig from a Tory.

Knowing he was headed for trouble, Brother Davey just up and played it bold. "I held me up a sack—shook 'er right in their faces, I did! 'Them hills over yonder's made outta that!' I told 'em. Which is th' gospel truth!"

Nobody, but *nobody*, would reveal such a secret, so the people scoffed. "An' whilst they was scoffin' I up 'n sneaked out—" But somebody did not scoff.

A short distance from the bar, Brother Davey was knocked from his horse, beaten, and left lying senseless on the dark, seldom-traveled road. "But," the Marshal rushed on when there was a rumble of fury at the loss of their gold, "the old gent fooled them all right. They took every bag, leaving only what was stitched inside his raincoat. The bags the hoodlums took were stuffed with river sand. The hills *are* full of that!"

His laugh broke the tension. A pause. Then the crowd joined him, their laughter reflecting such relief that the voices were high-pitched and unnatural with emotion.

The General and the Marshal were ready to abandon the search for Brother Davey and return with the sad news. Then Marshal Hunt visited Lucretia at the hospital and found Brother Davey—mumbling, rambling, but recognizing the Marshal enough to recall his own name and ask to be taken to his Emmy gal. On the way home, he had remembered more . . . but not the real enemy yet.

Oh, the *real* gold? Delivered. Assayed. Recorded— temporarily. Nothing definite until Cole's approval.

28

Missing Person

Men who seldom allowed their emotions to show gathered their families and pushed hurriedly through the doors of the Meeting House. In the sanctity of their humble cabins they would kneel in prayer. Brother Davey's safe return gave reason for gratitude. Cole's disappearance led to pleas for his safety. But with both incidents serving as grim reminders of life's fragility, they would devote most of the family worship to prayers for the safety of their own loved ones. Later they would offer help.

The building emptied quickly. Rachel, standing in the shadows near the front door, saw General Wilkes and Marshal Hunt making their way to her through the maze of rough-hewn benches, askew in the hurried exit. Now the room echoed every sound, spelling out desertion.

"Cole—you found no clue, did you?" Rachel's voice sounded hollow in her own ears.

And the General's voice, generally so deep with reassurance, sounded far away and uncertain. "I have something for you, but I beg of you not to take it as final—"

The roar in Rachel's ears became a living thing, its dark tentacles of despair gripping her heart. Squeezing it dry. How was it possible to think when life had gone from her body? And yet a part of Rachel was behaving normally. Preparing her for the words of finality from the military man who stood, unrecognizable, ready to deliver the message that the Angel of Death had delivered to so many women before her. Awaiting the words, she did not hear Buck enter.

We regret to inform you—

"No! Wait!" Buck's words boomed against the walls without meaning. He took her in his arms. Without meaning . . . *life* was without meaning . . . didn't he know?

She allowed Buck to hold her as the General put a small package in her hand. Cole's personal effects, he said. And, as if in a last rite, Rachel handed the package to Buck. "Open it."

"This could wait, Rachel. It isn't as if—"

"*Open* it!"

Cole's hat. A hunting knife. *His clothes!* And something cold, hard, metallic. The cross. Cole had taken it. Some far-off part of her wondered why.

Marshal Hunt was trying to reassure her. "We have ordered the militia out. *Find those men*, we told them, *find them in a hurry.*"

"Cole's murderers? Yes, find them," she said without inflection. It did not occur to her to ask how the men came to have her husband's effects.

"Rachel—Rachel! *Listen* to me!" Buck was shaking her gently. Her body was limp, as if without bones. "We have no proof that anything has happened to Cole. Foul play, yes. But Cole *dead*? We know better, Rachel. Not *dead*."

Dear Buck. Dear, wonderful Buck. Trying first to console her. Then shock her into reality.

"That's right, Mrs. Lord. He's only missing. I have worked with many of these cases. Always they strip away the identity. We'll find your husband." Marshal Hunt promised.

But why? Why, why, WHY?

There was discontent, misdirected hostility throughout the state, the men took turns explaining. Politics...somewhere subversive propaganda being printed. Somewhere a dozen cores of conspiracy politically and Cole was becoming a powerful name. The malcontents were embittered...the men who were failures...those who were deranged. Not an unfamiliar pattern until the government stabilized. And then there was the gold. There were rumors of a strike, the Lost Mine. But nobody *knew*...unless there was a spy among them. Indians unhappy on the reservation. Indians unhappy about the diggings on Superstition Mountain. *Any of these...*

But somewhere there was a leader. A leader who might act and talk like a puppet. Did Mrs. Lord have a photo of her husband?

Rachel pointed at the wall. Star's drawings bore a greater likeness than any photograph. Marshal Hunt took the pictures of Cole, nodding with satisfaction. Then pausing, he tore another picture from the wall quickly as if not to be observed. But Rachel saw. And a thrill of horror raced the length of her spine. Julius Doogan—and Star had added a beard!

29

The Testing

From that day forward little Star did not mention her father's name. It was as if she had crawled back into the world from which she had emerged—a world nobody else in the wagon train had known. A world in which she could hide. In it she could speak her native tongue, so that even in her prayers she was hidden.

Only Buck seemed able to coax an occasional word or phrase of English from the heartbroken child. She was abandoned, hurt, lonely, with all dreams rubbed out.

"I know the feeling, Lord. Oh, Lord, I know the feeling!" The words were wrenched from Rachel's heart over and over. To Buck she said, "How can I explain?"

"Let her be, Rachel," Buck said gently.

"But it's as if there's a wall between us when we should be so close. I can't even understand her prayers."

"God can," Buck said.

In her double loneliness, Rachel redoubled her

efforts to be the kind of teacher who could hold the villagers together through their children. Aunt Em had sown the seed with her Bible stories. Star, who now wished to be called Estrellita ("my real Spanish name"), had made the words come alive with her drawings. Now Rachel felt called upon to nourish the children's spiritual lives with the deeper meanings of the Bible. In the pursuit, the years rolled back to the Bible study and prayer around the camp fire on the Oregon Trail. It had held them together there. It could reunite them all once more. The Book of Love . . .

Then her heart would race, spin, and dance with joy. To be with Cole again under a sky full of stars . . . watching for a shooting star . . . such a tiny speck in the firmament . . . but one which could light the world . . .

She and Yolanda were turning pages rapidly in an effort to stay ahead of the children in a Bible-study treasure hunt when Rachel realized that a man was tapping on the newly-glassed window in front. The sight of the thickset man in his mid-50's frightened her. Then she realized that the children, so glee-filled in their word game, would have muffled a possible knock. A quick look, as she hurried to the door, showed an ancient bag in his hand. He held a worn book with one page turned down. Like the corners of his mouth, she thought.

"I'm Acting Superintendent of the public schools," he anounced upon entering, "Mr. Simon Netherton."

Either Mr. Simon Netherton did not see or chose to ignore Rachel's outstretched hand. He looked embittered, she thought. As if he carried some real or fancied grievance.

"I have come to examine the premises and to test your efficiency—both of you."

"Oh no!" Yolanda exclaimed. Then, reddening, she clapped both hands over her mouth.

"You would have done no better tomorrow."

"You are right," Yolanda said meekly before casting a desperate look at Rachel.

Rachel found herself able to turn palms up, a gesture the two girls had used since childhood to mean that the two of them had the advantage. Today was no exception. Rachel had noted, as the visiting superintendent set his bag and dog-eared book on her desk, that something about the place or herself intimidated the man. As a result, he held himself stiffly, on the defensive.

Ignoring Mr. Netherton's earlier rebuff, Rachel extended her hand. She was amused to see him unbend slightly, shake her hand, and voluntarily reach for Yolanda's.

As he pulled papers from his bag, Rachel found herself surprised at her own composure. She was beginning to realize that she was fully capable of coping with almost any situation now. *Was that,* she wondered with a stab of pain in her heart, *why the Lord had allowed her to fend for herself—then fend for others as well?*

The test was short. The visiting superintendent seemed suddenly in a hurry to be on his way. Only later did the two girls get what Yolanda called the "shakes."

"Had you not passed, Amity School would have gone unaccredited and been closed down. I bid you good day." With that, he was gone.

"The people couldn't have stood that—just one more shock would do them in." Yolanda's voice was trembling.

Rachel's weak knees buckled and she sat down on one of the split-log benches quickly. He asked so little about our qualifications—our personal lives." She took a deep breath. "Maybe I did wrong in not telling him I am expecting a child—and certainly I should have told you—"

"As I should have told you that I, too, am expecting. Expecting to be married, that is!"

Married? Surely she had misunderstood. But, no, Yolanda was going on. Not defensively exactly, Rachel thought. More as if to convince *herself*.

"I've learned that love rests on a sense of need. Like those pesky transitive verbs the children are struggling with. It requires an object! A husband and wife love each other because they *need* one another. Right?"

Rachel studied a moment. Then she answered carefully, "It depends on what you mean by *need*."

"Loving those who love *us*."

"Not according to the Bible, Yolanda. Otherwise, what reward have we?"

"Jesus wasn't talking about marriage!"

"I hope not." Rachel's voice was so low Yolanda did not hear. She, too, was guilty of marriage based on need.

"It's based on respect." Rachel nodded and Yolanda continued. "And on friendship—like you have with Buck."

Rachel stiffened. "I am unavailable. Who, Yolanda?"

• • •

When Buck came to walk with Rachel and Estrellita to Wednesday night prayer meeting, Rachel told him of Yolanda's plans to marry Timothy Norvall. Buck nodded absently and pointed out the North Star to Estrellita.

"Find the Big Dipper. I'm thirsty."

Estrellita giggled for the first time in ages.

"Make mine buttermilk if you're going by the Milky Way!"

Again the giggle.

"I appreciate your help with her so much," Rachel whispered as, wordlessly, Star's eyes searched the heavens.

"Hey, what are friends for?"

"That's what I was going to tell you—Yolanda's choice is based on what she called *need*. Then she translated it into friendship."

Buck took her arm. "Better than the ancient bride-price system, based on anything from the bride's education to her wealth. Wealth meaning—well, sometimes a few cows or dogs sufficed for a girl who could not so much as scrawl her name. I guess it depended on the father's values."

The past reached up and slapped Rachel across the face in the darkness. Her own price, money to support her father's appetite for rum, was more degrading. How *had* she and Cole survived?

She shivered against Buck. His hand tightened on her arm. "Yolanda will be all right. They have faith between them—and I guess Doogan was enough to wring the neck of any more romantic notions. Time will be the test."

Time. I, too, am being tested by time. The thought was frightening.

30

A Flicker of Hope

April came in, sweet-breathed and ruffling the valley with apple blossoms. Cole had said that apples bloomed out in the snow when he was with her. Rachel wondered now if he could smell them, remember, and know that she was remembering, too—wherever he was.

Four months had passed and there had been no word from him. Nothing from General Wilkes. Nothing from Marshal Hunt in spite of his promises. And nothing from the searching parties, the militia —nothing, nothing at all.

Even more disheartening was the fact that Rachel's letters went unanswered, although she had attempted to contact every group supposedly working in the still-new Bureau of Missing Persons. It was as if Cole had vanished in thin air. But that was impossible. Somebody knew *something*. The thought made her more intemperate in her demands for some kind of action, or at least a report, in her letters. All to no avail.

Rachel took to writing to Cole "General Delivery,"

mailing her daily letters to every post office Willie
Mead had listed on his newest pencil-sketch map.
When the letters came back marked "Unknown,"
she all but gave up hope.

But now it was Easter. The time of new beginnings. Surely something would happen to give her
hope.

And it did!

Timothy Norvall read the account of Jesus' death
and resurrection to a large congregation. People who
were unable to find seating space stood along the
walls. Then, when he began his sermon, men on the
outside poked their heads in through the windows,
fanning themselves with their hats between *Amens*.

The singing was louder, more victorious, than
Rachel could recall since earlier days in the settlement. The prayers more fervent. As if worship, like
talk of problems surrounding the valley, had been
too long restrained and now had found release. They
had all been so busy trying to put their lives together
again—hoping, while almost afraid to hope.

"Ye did a fine job, me lad. Never was to me likin'
t'see a job half-done—leavin' Jesus hangin' on th'
cross 'stead o'lettin' Him rise up in victory—"

Judson Lee's words were lost in the rumble of
carriage wheels. Faces went blank. Then, one by
one, eyes lost their glaze of fear and the settlers
turned one to the other with questioning faces.
There was dead silence.

When the carriage stopped, U.S. Marshal Hunt
tipped his hat, alighted, and turned to assist a single
passenger.

Lucretia!

But she was not the Lucretia the women (prisoners
of plainness and so hungry for beauty) remembered.
They noticed the change immediately. Her dress was
beaded in tawdy elegance. The beautiful raven

hair—once so sleek and shining—was frizzed in top-heavy curls, and a heavy layer of makeup was slathered on her face.

But Rachel was concentrating on the frightened eyes, the rigid body through which a powerful current seemed to be shooting. And the woman was clinging pitifully to the dusty armrest of the carriage, gritting her teeth, fighting back the telltale twitches and jerks that spelled hysteria.

Rachel moved forward. The other women followed. And somehow they managed to get Lucretia into the hotel. Her babbling made no sense. And the Marshal, his eyes bloodshot with weariness, was bent on explaining.

"It's not unusual, you know, women needing the pamperings they had back East. Love brings them here and loyalty keeps them. Then they shrivel. Mirrors are their enemies. . ."

"We understand, Marshal." Buck put a friendly arm around Marshal Hunt's shoulders. "You're among friends. Just tell us why you chose to bring your wife back. Then we will get on to other matters."

The Marshal gave him a look of gratitude. Then he looked at Lucretia. Confused, lost, defenseless, she looked like a frightened doe. "She insisted—and you must be the judge as to the—well, credibility of what she tells you—"

● ● ●

Think. I must have time to think. Alone. . .
Then one week later Rachel came out of her self-exile. She must coax something—*anything*—from Brother Davey.

After her one burst of seemingly lucid information, Lucretia went into a coma of silence. She refused to talk even to her husband, picked at her food, and sat staring into space. Then Marshal Hunt asked Yolanda to stay with her one evening while he drew the men together, and then he took her back to the sanitorium under construction in Portland. Maybe the new surroundings would help...he would be back.

But Rachel hardly heard. She must compare stories—*now*!

Aunt Em welcomed her with open arms. "Been mighty sick, he has. Don't go gettin' yourself alarmed if he goes outta his head sort of. Here, sit down, you're white as a flour sack. I oughta be givin' you this care—and you in a family way 'n all, dearie." Aunt Em pushed her into a chair.

Brother Davey raised himself on elbow, kicking back the bed covers. "Give th' little darlin' some o'this witch's potion. It'll git her misery over—one way or t'other—"

"Ain't what goes into th' mouth that's defilin', Davey love—it's what comes out! I know it's delirium, but—"

Brother Davey snorted. "They kept me down under with them sleepin' powders—me'n Miz Lucretia—and now you with this catnip 'n slippery elm. Something's bound t'be comin' outta my mouth. I'm rememberin'! Why, that crum', that bum, that *scum*!"

"Let him talk," Rachel whispered, feeling a first flicker of hope.

31

The Reality of a Dream

Where does one draw the fine line between reality and a dream? Rachel lay across her bed, her eyes closed against the red-orange bar of light slanting through the window, the sun's farewell to another day.

Who was to say whether Lucretia was bordering on insanity? Or that Brother Davey was still dazed from the beating he had taken along the road? Parts of their strange stories made sense, a fact one might ignore, except that at points their accounts coincided, their corners meeting and overlapping. That *had* to mean something. But what? "Oh, dear God, You spoke to me once—now *show* me—"

When there was a rap at the door, Rachel ignored it as she had ignored other knocks and calls which would have invaded the privacy of her thinking. But she did open her eyes. And what she saw made her catch her breath. In the half-dark, she could see the outline of Cole's face in the cheval mirror. Any moment he would reach down to coil his fingers in her hair. But no, he was motioning...and she, closing her eyes again, stepped over the time zone of the present...

• • •

From far downriver to the south there came the muffled sound of a single horse's hoofs. Light-stepping as if to ferry its rider secretly through the night. And then the sound changed as the great black stallion (*Hannibal, of course*) set foot on the loose-boarded bridge linking the narrow road leading from the settlement to the main road. Across a sea of snow, the horse and rider, silhouetted starkly against an island of trees, were clearly visible. The man sat stiffly erect. Listening. Looking. *Cole!*

Rachel wanted to cry out a warning. But, behind closed eyelids, she saw him vanish in the wooded area. And then the sound of horses' hooves—a hundred surely—told her that others had caught sight of the passerby.

Something was wrong. Very wrong. Cole who had gone to rescue Brother Davey, was now to be taken prisoner himself. It was as if Rachel knew before it happened. And there was nothing she could do. Except watch the story unfold, filling in the missing scraps of the pattern Brother Davey and Lucretia had begun then found themselves short on material...

Cole squinted against the gray darkness of the small room—his mind fogged with sedation, yet feeling beneath it anger and frustration. With an effort, he reached to touch his clothes. Gone, just as he suspected—as were his wallet, his hunting knife, and the cross he had brought along on im-pulse in order to hold something of Rachel close to his heart. A messenger in case...

"My hat!" He had hoped to yell the words, but the dryness of his throat throttled them to a thirsty whisper. "My cross—to my wife—my *hat!*"

"Settle down. You're going nowhere."

The graying man in a white coat meant to be kind. It was only that he didn't understand that whoever waylaid Cole had taken a gold nugget as well as the list of shareholders to the mine tucked inside the sweat brim of his hat. What pack of savages had jumped him in the dark?

"How did I come to be here?" he asked weakly.

The man, whose back was to him, reached for a stethoscope and shrugged. "We may never know. I am only a doctor. Lie still."

Was there fear in his voice? Cole followed the man's eyes to the shadowy figure in the doorway.

"I know that man—I know him!" The voice was high-pitched and, for a moment, help seemed near. Maybe the woman in the filmy night garment could furnish him an anchor.

But no. Somebody was dragging her away. It was time for her tincture of opium, they said.

"Isn't that stuff powerful?" Cole spoke rapidly. "Doctor, couldn't I see her before she's under?"

Again the shrug. And there was caution in his voice when at length he spoke.

"I've no power here. I go strictly by the book—*my* book." He held up a worn copy of *Updated Medical Reference*. "But," lowering his voice, "she's in the next room. By the way, we'll need your name."

Cole breathed so deeply it hurt his chest. He had nothing—*nothing*—to prove that he was Colby Lord. Unless—

• • •

(I recognized him from the pictures the little Indian girl drew. "Mexican," Rachel had wanted to correct Lucretia but dared not interrupt. *I thought he could help me—until I saw what trouble he was in . . . oh, what trouble! They kept bringing him forms, saying he wasn't who he claimed—he wasn't anybody at all until he could fill out all those papers. He wanted to get some letters out, but he had no stamps or paper and would I lend him some? I did—just in time, too. They surrounded the place with guards . . . hand me my headache pills, somebody.)*

● ● ●

The medicine the doctor gave Cole was beginning to take effect. He managed to get a letter to Rachel completed, but for the coded psalm. Then he was surrounded by overly-polite faces. They would get him a new identity. Yes, he *must* have an identity. No amount of reasoning made any difference. *Just sign here, sir.* Over and over they handed him a pencil which he managed to drop, feigning sleep. *Sign?* By what name?

Just sign here. Then he would be entitled to nothing. *Just swear that there has been a mistake and we will let you go.* Wasn't that what they promised? But this was a hospital. He was free to leave. Wasn't he?

Sleep pulled at his eyelids, pushed down on his brain. That was when he shakily made his way to Lucretia Hunt's room carrying the letter he wanted mailed to Rachel.

He did not linger. A shuffle of footsteps warned him to hurry back to his room. And just in time. A man entered to bring Cole a meal. Cold beans. Undercooked. Cole pushed them away.

"If you'll bring me my clothes—"

The man pinched his glasses tighter on his ferret-like nose. His mouth sank in as if he wore no teeth.

"Your personal effects have been turned over to the authorities. As to your leaving," he said, picking up the untouched bowl of beans, "it will be up to the judge."

The judge?

Yes, the closest thing to the law here. Fact was, he *was* the law—you know, settling gambling disputes, claims, nabbing claim jumpers, and performing marriages. But biggest penalty of all for the claim jumping, usually under an assumed name.

Cole was beginning to understand. But when he would have asked more questions, the ferret-faced man stopped him.

"Save your questions for the judge. You'll see him come tomorrow. You're being transferred tonight."

"I don't even know where I am now—"

"Don't really matter. We took over. Will at Blue Bucket, too."

• • •

(I heard him screaming, "It matters—it matters!" Lucretia remembered with a shudder. *They beat him. It was like I could hear their knuckle bones crushing his skull or jaw. I guess they killed him because the groans all stopped. I tried to ask, but they said I was imagining things—in need of my medicine, like I am now . . .")*

• • •

Aware of a stabbing behind his eyes, Cole stirred on the hard dirt floor. Even before the mud-chinked walls of the drafty lean-to came into focus, something warned him. And the bars at the sawed-out squares serving for windows said he was right. He was in jail!

His vision was still blurred when someone rattled the chain securing the door and stepped inside. Unable to make out more than the outline of a man, Cole waited for some identifying sound.

"Did you sleep well, Mr. Lord?"

Oh, the hateful sneer of the remembered voice!

"What am I doing here? What are *you* doing here, Doogan?"

"*Judge* Doogan!" The voice italicized the title in warning. "People are lucky to have somebody to take over when all records were destroyed—*including* ownership of Blue Bucket!"

Careful. Humor him. Stay calm. Fragments of memory, like warning lights, flashed before Cole's eyes: ". . . You'll pay for this, Colby Lord—you and your bought-and-paid-for, high-and-mighty bride." . . . Julius Doogan's threat at the Blue River crossing.

"If you refer to the division in the wagon train on the trail, I did what I had to do."

"*Had to do!*" Julius Doogan's voice rose. Like a knife, the words cut through the distance between the two men. "Just as I did. We had the same purpose—gold! I *knew* about the mine."

Cole swallowed in an effort to get the words from his dry throat with a false civility. "I came to make application to plat out a city once the charter was granted—" Cole paused, struck by a sudden idea. "You are in a position to help me now, Julius—"

"*Judge* to you. I try, sentence, and execute!"

Flatter him. Anything to soothe him. Obviously, the man was mad.

"You've come a long way," Cole said thickly, the words knotting in his throat. "You must know the right people—you could help get me out of here—"

It was then that Julius, the half-beaten enemy,

leaped over Cole's still-limp body, and stood looking into his face, wild-eyed. "*Help* you! I'm the one who *put* you here!"

Cole made one more try. "It's Brother Davey—"

Julius Doogan laughed unpleasantly. "Some mission—better be concerning yourself with your own! Your wife's as desirable as ever." His laugh was insulting. "Expecting another baby, you know—"

Rachel...Rachel's dream had come true. Oh, Rachel!

"So if you plan on being there, you'd better make no false moves. No trying for escape—you're being watched. Just sign over the claims to me as owner and get out of here. You see—" Julius's voice was suddenly low, suggestive, "you never can tell who the father is—"

With all the frail strength left in his weakened body, Cole grasped at the legs standing so close. Julius Doogan swore. Then Cole felt the heavy heel of a boot crushing the pit of his stomach. He gasped and opened his mouth, knowing he was going to be sick. He imagined he heard voices before he lost consciousness, but he could never be sure...

• • •

(*That polecat! That wrung-neck goose! I hope th' Lord shows no mercy on him!* Aunt Em had had to threaten Brother Davey with another dram of catnip and no more talking to calm him. *Did'n thank I'd know 'im with that beard...and fer a spell I didn'n. Kept askin' 'bout Cole and forcing that sleep-stuff down my gullet, so's I was outta my mind. I heard th' beatin' I did—in th' hospital. Then, sudden-like, I was in a shed that looked like 'twas put together* *by a dirt dobber. Then I heared that voice—only I was so befuddled I could'n help Cole. Not even when that scum callin' hisself "judge" said they needed no jury—lawbreakers like 'im—murderers 'n claim jumpers'd be tried, found guilty, 'n swung from th' hangin' tree...I recall 'n wisht I did'n...*Brother Davey had leaned harder against his pillow and closed his eyes. Rachel saw a weak tear trickle down his cheek.)

• • •

How long was he there? Cole was unable to tell one day from another—or even the turning of the seasons. His hair grew long on his neck. And once, because there was a cinder in his eye, someone brought him a jagged piece off a broken mirror. In it, he saw a gaunt face, the matted hair around it threaded with gray. *His* face? Surely not. Not even a member of the human race.

Because the thought of today would drive him stark raving mad, he tried to think of the morrow. There could be no mail. No contact of any kind with the outside world. And when his mind began to wander dangerously, Colby Lord would think of the future...his Rachel...their dreams. Enlarged now to include the child they wanted so much...

Only there could be no future. He would die and rot here before he would swear to some lie that would rob his faithful friends of their rights to Blue Bucket Mine.

Anger would take over then and he would beat on the walls until someone came. The same questions. The same threats to him and his family. And finally a deathblow in the face which was almost a relief. It blacked out the desolate world.

He hardly knew when they took him away.

• • •

(*They come t'take me back to th' hospital, seein'
I knowed nothin'. An' that's where th' Marshal
found me. . .but*—Brother Davey tugged at his side-
whiskers—*but not before I seen 'em totin' him
away. . .then there was scramblin', screamin', 'n
yellin'. . .Indians? Can't rightly say. But—But—oh,
yes, I recollect now. Th' Gen'ral come. . .maybe after
Cole was gone. . .th' military. . .an' sayin' how no
self-anointed*—"Appointed, Davey love," Aunt Em
corrected—*yeah, that, too. Sech wasn't a-gonna have
no jury. . .no 'twasn't jury—juryis, juris*—"Jurisdiction?"—*jurisdiction under th' law. . .*)

• • •

Faces swam before him. They must have split his
head in half. One part was jubilant. The other was
witless. Desperately he fought to realign his
thinking.

"You mean I'm free to go?" Even as he asked, Cole
felt the old sense of foreboding. Another trick. Oh,
thank God, he had not allowed Rachel—darling Rachel who was carrying his child—to come. How
many months had it been now? Long enough for him
to forget how to listen. For words the man standing
over him, wearing polished boots—and the fringe
swinging near his face as the hands lifted him must
have been on his gloves—was saying made no sense.

Yes. Yes—and no. He was free as freedom went. But
—and the words ran together like the faces behind
the speaker—". . .protective custody. . .material wit-
ness. . .problem being that nobody—*nobody* must
know he was alive. *Family?* No! Family last of
all. They were being watched. . .watched *over*

as well...time...it would take time." *These were friends?*

• • •

(*So they kept somebody. Cole? No, don't rightly think so—but my brain's been churnin' like 'twas tryin' fer buttermilk*...Brother Davey had drifted away again.)

32

"And Does Not Swear Deceitfully"

Again the knocking. This time accompanied by a voice.

"Let me in, Rachel! Rachel—Rachel, are you all right?"

Was she all right? Rachel was not sure. Somehow, during the long journey, for surely it had been a journey of the mind—Rachel had slid from the bed and onto her knees beside it. Her prayer must have been very long because now she was unable to move. Her head was whirling like a spinning jenny, taking everything in the room with it. Her face was lifted upward, but her body had dissolved.

"*Rachel!*" This time Buck's voice carried a command, a command she tried to obey, pushing up on wobbly legs.

When her fumbling hands managed to unbolt the door, she fell against Buck, who was quick to support her weight and guide her back to the bed. Her body was sweat-soaked, but her eyes were as dry as coins. She tried for a voice.

"Buck, oh, Buck," she gasped.

And then she told him her story. When she turned to him, her eyes were brimming. "Do you suppose —is there a chance—?"

Buck propped a pillow beneath her head then brought her a glass of water. "I don't know, Rachel," he said gently. "I, too, have heard reports." He hesitated and then said, "But we must remember all this would have been some time ago. And even if Cole were safe, he'd have been back to us by this time."

"In case he's free, completely free."

And then she remembered the letter. Cole's only letter. The letter she had read and pondered over, praying each night for an interpretation. What if this were in answer?

Springing from the bed with renewed energy, she ran to pick up Cole's family Bible. His letter served as a bookmark. The first part was too personal to share, but it was the quotation from the Bible she wanted Buck to hear.

"Listen!" And Rachel read the passage from Psalms aloud, then waited for Buck's reaction. There was none.

"Don't you see?" Her voice was almost desperate. "And who shall stand in his holy place? He who has clean hands and a pure heart, *who does not lift up his soul to what is false, and does not swear deceitfully.*"

Buck sat for a long time with his eyes closed as if trying to see what Rachel had seen. When at last he looked up, there was a strange look about him.

"Rachel, think hard. Did Lucretia or Brother Davey mention someone's trying to force a signature—or was that a part of your—?"

"Imagination? Oh, Buck, it was more—"

Buck nodded. "I wasn't going to say that. What we call it doesn't matter. I believe you."

Rachel wanted to throw her arms around him in appreciation. Instead, she sat very still, hands knotted in her lap. His next words could be critical.

But they weren't. Not in the way she expected anyway.

"Did Burt Clemmons bring Cole's hat back?"

"Cole's hat? Why, I never knew he took it. When and for what purpose?" Glancing at the peg where Cole had always hung the hat and she had replaced it when it was returned to her, Rachel saw that it was no longer there.

"I didn't know Burt had been back."

"Only long enough to tack up the pictures in the post office. He asked my permission about the hat and pictures."

Rachel nodded, remembering that copies of Estrellita's drawings had been scattered throughout the region. Cole's on the flyer about a MISSING PERSON caption. Julius Doogan's two (the one drawn long ago, another with a disguising beard) beneath the words, WANTED, DEAD OR ALIVE.

"I think," Buck said, spacing each word carefully, "that we will not be satisfied unless I myself have searched for Cole . . ."

33

No More Tears

Rachel did not weep when Buck returned with no news of Cole. She had cried too long. Too hard. For too many years. Now there were no tears in reserve. She felt the long, fleshless fingers of something nameless clutch her heart. Death? No, she could not think of Cole—wonderful, vital, empire-building Cole—as dead. Neither must she think of him as alive.

Somewhere she heard a meadowlark's call. And in the tall fir trees beyond her window the wind continued its tireless play. Life lay in Cole's dreams. If they lived, he lived. And as long as he lived, so did she. Think of Estrellita...think of the baby...of the town.

Rachel reached for and found a thin layer of sanity, pulling it gently about her...

Buck had better sense than to try to comfort her now. Instead, he told her that he had been able to make all the proper contacts. Would she believe that all the vital information for replacing claims destroyed in the floods had been tucked inside the sweatband of Cole's hat?

Yes, she would believe. The explanation to all this lay in the dream. Only it wasn't a dream. A dream revolves around the dreamer, and Rachel's vision had included Cole and the enemy. She wasn't there. It did not matter now. Oh, yes, it mattered! It *had* to...

And so she listened to Buck. "All's in order—grants, deeds, everything. We can begin as soon as they are here..."

• • •

Like a melting glacier, life crawled on. May moved over for June. The mantles of snow grew more and more narrow, finally disappearing completely from the shoulders of the mountains to add new strength to the swollen river. Enough rain fell to unlock the entire earth, decorating it with emerald beards of spring wheat, promising abundant harvests.

In July the promised papers came. Along with them, the draft from the bank. Now came the decisions. The men met and puzzled over all the paperwork. On Sunday afternoons, while "walking off" their heavy dinner, they stepped off the ground: this for farming, that for the extension of the city. Questions were, Did they want to pursue the mining? Could be the mountain furnished just one rich vein. Or, did they want to return to farming the rich, virgin soil? Either way, the town was going to be built as platted. And the "non-denominational church" was first on the list.

Rachel walked with them sometimes, her body weighted, her heart leaden. But she did not weep...

34

Lordsburg

A new kind of prosperity set in. Business had never been better in the hotel. Brother Davey, having regained his strength and part—if not all—of his memory, pitched in with a new zeal to help Aunt Em. Every day a larger number of wagons rumbled into the village. Laden with all their worldly goods, the families, still gold-hungry, followed rumors of new strikes. "Still pots of gold at the end of the rainbow," they said, wolfing down Aunt Em's sourdough biscuits. Brother Davey looked doubtful but, under his wife's watchful eye, said nary a word about Oregon's rainbows betwixt sun and showers. And never, ever did his eye stray to the sealed-off mine atop Superstition Mountain. Let them travel on to the California fields. So the "Lost Mine" *was* lost—in conversation and in a whorl of fog.

The other men divided their time between their harvest (maturing and finding a ready market) and building. Hammers and saws rang out and echoed against the canyon walls to blend with the whistling and singing of those who manned them. Signs were repainted as, one by one, stores reopened to boast of newer and better merchandise.

Outside the village, Rachel watched cabins begin to take shape. One wall...two...and finally four, as laboriously the mules snaked logs down from the hills. She had no interest in proceeding with the building of, or even talking about, the great house Cole had sketched. A house, even if it had a marble floor, would be nothing more. Just a house. Not a *home*.

And even as the other settlers chatted, worked, planned, and sang hymns of praise, she felt a certain air of tentativeness. Were they awaiting final notice of their leader's death? Or could it be that they held out hope? Surely they could not be biding their time until official word came that Blue Bucket Mine could be reopened. When, having done their "duty" here, they could swarm back in search of what she saw as man's mortal enemy—gold. Couldn't they see what it had done already?

Gold had robbed her of the most precious thing in the world—her husband. Gold had taken Estrellita away in spirit. Gold had left her alone to bear a child. Bitterly, Rachel wished the Lord would turn the earth upside down and empty its pockets of the gold they held.

Immediately she was sorry. After all, these were Cole's loyal friends. Salt-of-the-earth people. God's people seeing that Cole's dream took shape, even though (as they phrased it in their conversations with her) he was "away."

General Wilkes, followed by what appeared to be a dozen men in uniform, rode into the village on July Fourth. Rachel shaded her eyes, hoping against hope. But it had grown hotter. Hot winds whipped through the gap, drawing a dry aroma from the dying weeds and sighing pine trees. Dust swirled, obscuring the hard, once-brilliant disk of sun. Dust swirled and eddied before her eyes.

The General had alighted and was holding both her hands before Rachel's vision cleared. "My dear— so lovely as always. And so brave!" His kind eyes swept her swollen body.

"Oh, General—please—*please*—is there news?"

Of course, there was news. But Rachel knew such men did not play games. He would come right to the point.

"I wish there were something I could tell you, my dear child. I would not be at liberty even were there something I knew. Such information is highly classified. But note that the pictures are down."

When Rachel asked why, General Wilkes did not answer. And the moment was lost. Others were gathering, each with a million questions. No more pictures, no more searching. . .?

"Patience," he said with a smile which demonstrated the word. "Let's gather in the Meeting House to get Mrs. Lord from this broiling sun. Oh, what progress you have made. Why, you've done wonders! And so many new faces—" The General walked toward the Meeting House as he talked.

"Your men will be hungry, Gen'ral, Sir—needin' refreshment?" Aunt Em's question was hopeful.

He smiled. "Refreshment, yes—and lodging for a time. It seems best with all the unrest."

"Should be we meet in th' church yonder soon," Judson Lee pointed with pride to the only building smartly covered with shake siding. "Remember me? I'm duly elected Lord Mayor—"

The General suppressed a smile. "Nice, very nice indeed. And you'll be receiving the makings of a belfry. You do have a piano?"

Oh, yes, indeed, someone was saying. One with

a new leg. That the "piano" was a harpsichord made no difference.

Indeed, the air was cooler. The General told of some of the changes. Old Oregon was gone for good—or should one say "for worse," there being so many undesirables coming, looting, shooting... but there was progress...applications made for establishment of a bank...a doctor...

At last he came to the point. "Portland or Oregon city may neither be the state capital, after all. Champoeg was washed away in the flood, you know, destroying all records there. And it is my studied opinion that Lafayette is as big today as it will be 100 years hence. Sooooo...there's every possibility that the city you are helping Colby Lord to complete could be—"

He was interrupted by cheering. At length, the General held up his hand. "First, a name—a permanent one."

"Lee's Landing...Galloway Gap...Cole's Valley ...*Lordsburg*...yes, Lordsburg, that would be th' best..."

Lordsburg. Rachel had listened to the chant of suggestions quietly. Now she felt a stir of emotion. There was something sad about the name. It was like a memorial, a shrine.

Unless—Rachel suddenly was on her feet. "I must object." Her voice was loud and clear. "Cole traveled against impossible odds to build a city, but never once did he travel alone. Almighty God was beside him—and to Him goes the glory. The city will be a fulfillment of Cole's dream. But it is a fulfillment of God's purpose. The green pastures, and still waters. A city of God. Yes, Lordsburg if—if you mean the City of the Lord!"

There was a shout of praise, followed by another. The settlers understood. Led by Timothy Norvall, the men walked to the altar. And there they knelt in silent prayer.

* * *

It was too hot to eat inside, the women agreed. So by the time Rachel joined them, they were spreading a white cloth on the ground in the grove by the cemetery and laying out hot breads, freshly-churned butter, boiled eggs, chicken and dumplings, and wild strawberry pie. The air filled up with children's shrieks and laughter. But Estrellita's voice was not among them.

Rachel's heart skipped a beat. She must find her!

And then she saw the tiny figure bent low over the tiniest of the graves on the grassy slope, frail shoulders convulsing in sobs. Rachel stooped awkwardly to draw the child to her swollen body. Estrellita clung to her.

"God may want our baby for an angel—like Lorraine?"

"This is His city, too—Lordsburg," she soothed. *And in it you have come back to me in a language I can understand...*

35

A Time To Be Born

The youngest Lord chose her own time to be born. Due, the best Rachel and Aunt Em could calculate, in late September, Mary Cole bounced into the world on an early August midnight—unassisted.

"Go for Aunt Em, darling!" Rachel, clutching her middle with the first pang of warning, instructed Estrellita.

In her excitement, Estrellita stopped by to tell "Uncle Buck." And by the time the three of them, all half-clothed, were back, mother and baby were doing well!

"A mite in a hurry," Aunt Em said as she fussed over the baby's first oil rub.

"Are you anointing her, Grandma Emma?" Estrellita, all eyes, wanted to know.

"Could be—just could be—" Aunt Em answered absently. But it was plain to see that she was checking the plump, well-developed body, counting the ten pink fingers and toes. "A little beauty, she is— mostly like her mama 'ceptin' for that square jawline. Gonna have a mind of her own one day!"

And the prediction was fast in coming. Buck, who had stood by helplessly—first on one foot then the other, clenching and unclenching his hands repeatedly—was the first to scoop the baby up when she whimpered as Aunt Em placed her beside her mother.

That set the pattern. It was plain to see that Buck and Estrellita had taken over.

"Well, dearie, 'twas you who done it—you 'n Cole 'n th' Lord Hisself."

Rachel could not answer for the lump in her throat. Aunt Em, trying hard to swallow the lump in her own, went on talking. "Ain't it all just wonderful?" She smiled mischievously. "Only person I know what's bound on disappointment is Aggie. Little Mary Cole there's bearin' no markin's from th' raven or the fire!"

Rachel turned over and, with a tired smile, slept— little knowing that with a woman like Agnes Grant there had to be trouble. If none surfaced, she would keep dipping beneath the placid waters until there was something—*anything*—to change the pattern.

• • •

A chance remark (a "chance remark" well-planned!) did just that. "Colby Lord ain't a-comin' back, if you ask me—else he'd a-been here when his wife was a-needin' 'im. S'pose he's gone back East. Some men ain't satisfied with jest one job done—er with jest one woman fer that matter. Course Miz Lord's got herself grounds fer a divorcement if he's violated th' marriage bed—"

36

In His Time

Repeated more out of concern than malice, the words eventually reached Rachel. But somehow they felt familiar, as if she herself may have thought them. And then her heart would cry out to dispute such wild imaginings. *Forgive me, Lord!*

During the days that followed, she was so busy that she could control the ugliness of the thoughts. But nights, even with her daughters—more precious than life itself—close to her, she was lonely. Lonely and afraid.

And then the dream came. Startling at first. More startling when it paraded behind her closed eyelids with alarming regularity . . . and frighteningly like Mrs. Grant's whisperings . . .

At first, Rachel fancied herself dying, then dead. It was almost pleasant, floating as she was on the mists of some invisible cloud. Until her breathing stopped. She could not call out. But she could see, dimly at first, then more clearly—until at last the phantom became Cole.

Cole! Rachel longed to cry out but could not.

Suspended above him as she was, she could only watch as one watches a play in which the stage manager tells the story.

Cole stood on the little knoll they knew so well. His face looked lean, hardened, skin drawn tightly across his high cheekbones as if there were no flesh beneath. *Time*, she thought sadly, *the fingers of time had done that*. His eyes searched for, but did not find, her face. Would time have changed her, too? Was the bloom of youth gone? Did her eyes reveal the terminal bruise of her heart? Whatever he saw made him sad. Could he for one moment think she would have had him declared dead...gone on with another life? That the city was no longer his...that *she* was not his? Or was he bidding them all farewell?

For less time than her first conscious breath took as she awoke, Rachel tried to reach out, cry out, touch him. At first, the room was filled with the nearness. Then nothing remained. Except hope. Hope that tonight the dream would return, giving her a vision of its ending. Or did she wish to know?

• • •

September came with a burst of color. Then the leaves faded. And with them, her dream. Mary Cole rounded out like a dumpling...the belfry was mounted on the church and there was talk of a dedication. And all the while Yolanda was planning her wedding, begging Rachel and Buck to stand up with her and Timothy. But Rachel held back. It might give a wrong impression, she tried to explain. Wait...just wait a while for a final answer.

• • •

And then the waiting ended.

It was Estrellita who saw him first. Her voice, usually so musically soft, was high-pitched as she ran across the meadow of new-mown hay toward the knoll where Cole stood transfixed, surveying the changes spread before him.

"You never runned away!" Looking for the world like a straw-stuffed doll whose insides were falling out, Estrellita reached brown arms upward.

Cole never "runned away." Rachel stood statue-still, remembering the little child's story of desertion by her natural father. But Cole had not deserted his family. Had she ever truly thought he would—or that Cole, being Cole, *could?* And yet she could not move. It was too much. Too soon. She must sort the real from the dream...

And then she was being crushed by the dearly familiar arms. The face was not gaunt or the skin stretched. He looked fit. He looked beautiful. He looked wonderful. The only hungry-looking thing being his eyes that were coming closer and closer. And then when his lips touched hers, Rachel knew it was not a dream. Why, then, was she crying harder than Mary Cole when she demanded to be picked up?

"Never mind, Mother Mine, Daddy," Estrellita said, wedging herself between them. "She only cries when she is happy—and oh, oh, *oh*, so do *you!*"

Tonight beneath a harvest moon they would walk and talk, comparing the revelations of her dreams with what happened. Rachel sensed there would be a parallel, proving her dreams a revelation. The sign she had asked God to send her. Except for the last dream. That was induced by the evil of Mrs. Grant's prattling tongue...

They would look together at the peak of Superstition Mountain reaching upward into the cumulus clouds which, perhaps, were lined with gold. And they would talk about what to recommend. To explore the mountain's secrets. Or to leave its mysteries sealed off, letting it remain forever the "Lost Mine" that other generations would seek one day.

The waters of the life-giving river would burble softly beside them, pledging itself anew to green pastures—and eternal power. The seasons would come and go—each spring opening new buds of promise, each fall ripening their love.

But for now Cole must see his daughter. The gift from God Who made everything beautiful—*in His time.*